"A breathtaking tale...I absolutely loved it!"
    –Romance Junkies on Dark Craving, Dark Kings Series

"The author has created a fantastic and mesmerizing fantasy world with intriguing twists, surprises and unique elements that keeps the reader turning the pages to the very end."
    –Night Owl Reviews on Dark Heat, Dark Kings Series

"Evie and Malcolm is a couple that makes it impossible not to love them."
    –The Jeep Diva, Dark Warriors Series

"Grant's smoldering seventh Dark Warrior outing will grip readers from the first page, immersing them in her wounded, lonely couple's journey of redemption…each scene is filled with Grant's clever, complex characters and trademark sizzle."
    –Romantic Times Magazine (RT Book Reviews), Dark Warriors Series

DON'T MISS THESE OTHER SPELLBINDING NOVELS

BY NYT & USA TODAY BESTSELLING AUTHOR DONNA GRANT

CONTEMPORARY PARANORMAL

DRAGON KINGS SERIES

(Spin off series from **DARK KINGS SERIES**)

Book 1: Dragon Revealed (novella)

REAPER SERIES

Book 1: Dark Alpha's Claim

Book 2: Dark Alpha's Embrace

Book 3: Dark Alpha's Demand

Books 1-3 Bundle: Tall Dark Deadly Alpha

Book 4: Dark Alpha's Lover

Book 5: Dark Alpha's Night

Book 6: Dark Alpha's Hunger

Book 7: Dark Alpha's Awakening

Book 8: Dark Alpha's Redemption

Book 9: Dark Alpha's Temptation

Book 10: Dark Alpha's Caress

Book 11: Dark Alpha's Obsession

DARK KINGS SERIES

Book 16: Fever

Book 16.5: Dragon Lost (novella)

Book 17: Flame

Book 18: Inferno

The Dragon King Coloring Book

Dragon King Special Edition Character Coloring Book: Rhi

Book 19: Whisky and Wishes, A Dark Kings Special Holiday Novella

Book 20: Heart of Gold, A Dark Kings Special Valentine's Novella

Book 21: Of Fire and Flame

DARK WARRIORS SERIES

Book 1: Midnight's Master

Book 2: Midnight's Lover

Book 3: Midnight's Seduction

Book 4: Midnight's Warrior

Book 5: Midnight's Kiss

Book 6: Midnight's Captive

Book 7: Midnight's Temptation

Book 8: Midnight's Promise

Book 8.5: Midnight's Surrender (novella)

CHIASSON SERIES

Book 1: Wild Fever

Book 2: Wild Dream

Book 3: Wild Need

Book 4: Wild Flame

Book 5: Wild Rapture

LARUE SERIES

Book 1: Moon Kissed

Book 2: Moon Thrall

Book 3: Moon Struck

Book 4: Moon Bound

WICKED TREASURES

Book 1: Seized by Passion

Book 2: Enticed by Ecstasy

Book 3: Captured by Desire

Books 1-3: Wicked Treasures Box Set

HISTORICAL PARANORMAL

THE KINDRED SERIES

Book 0.5: Everkin (short story)

Book 1: Eversong

Book 2: Everwylde

Book 3: Everbound

Book 4: Evernight

Book 5: Everspell

DARK SWORD SERIES

Book 1: Dangerous Highlander

Book 2: Forbidden Highlander

Book 3: Wicked Highlander

Book 4: Untamed Highlander

Book 5: Shadow Highlander

Book 6: Darkest Highlander

ROGUES OF SCOTLAND SERIES

Book 1: The Craving

Book 2: The Hunger

Book 3: The Tempted

Book 4: The Seduced

Books 1-4: Rogues of Scotland Box Set

THE SHIELDS SERIES

Book 1: A Dark Guardian

Book 2: A Kind of Magic

Book 3: A Dark Seduction

Book 4: A Forbidden Temptation

Book 5: A Warrior's Heart

Mystic Trinity (a series connecting novel)

DRUIDS GLEN SERIES

Book 1: Highland Mist

Book 2: Highland Nights

Book 3: Highland Dawn

Book 4: Highland Fires

Book 5: Highland Magic

Mystic Trinity (a series connecting novel)

SISTERS OF MAGIC TRILOGY

Book 1: Shadow Magic

Book 2: Echoes of Magic

Book 3: Dangerous Magic

Books 1-3: Sisters of Magic Box Set

THE ROYAL CHRONICLES NOVELLA SERIES

Book 1: Prince of Desire

Book 2: Prince of Seduction

Book 3: Prince of Love

Book 4: Prince of Passion

Books 1-4: The Royal Chronicles Box Set

Mystic Trinity (a series connecting novel)

MILITARY ROMANCE / ROMANTIC SUSPENSE

SONS OF TEXAS SERIES

Book 1: The Hero

Book 2: The Protector

Book 3: The Legend

Book 4: The Defender

Book 5: The Guardian

COWBOY / CONTEMPORARY

HEART OF TEXAS SERIES

Book 1: The Christmas Cowboy Hero

Book 2: Cowboy, Cross My Heart

Book 3: My Favorite Cowboy

Book 4: A Cowboy Like You

Book 5: Looking for a Cowboy

Book 6: A Cowboy Kind of Love

STAND ALONE BOOKS

Mutual Desire

Forever Mine

Savage Moon

Dark Beginnings: A First in Series Boxset

Contains:

Chiasson Series, Book 1: Wild Fever

LaRue Series, Book 1: Moon Kissed

The Royal Chronicles Series, Book 1: Prince of Desire

Check out Donna Grant's Online Store for autographed books, character themed goodies, and more!

DARK ALPHA'S CARESS

REAPERS

DONNA GRANT

DARK ALPHA'S CARESS
© 2020 by DL Grant, LLC
Cover Design © 2020 by Charity Hendry
Formatting © 2020 by Charity Hendry

Excerpt from: **DARK ALPHA'S OBSESSION**
© 2020 by DL Grant, LLC

ISBN 13: 978-1942017622
Available in ebook, audio, and print editions.

www.DonnaGrant.com
www.MotherofDragonsBooks.com

CHAPTER ONE

Ballycastle, Ireland
July

She had officially lost her mind. That was the only thing she could think of that would have taken her from her home on the Isle of Skye and brought her to Northern Ireland. Sorcha wasn't exactly courageous. In fact, she considered herself a hermit.

But because she preferred to be alone, it made it easier for her to do precisely what she was currently doing.

"Rhona, you owe me big for this," she mumbled to herself as she walked the hilly landscape toward the coast.

The wind whipped her hair from its braid and into her eyes. She pulled the strands out of her lashes and tucked them behind her ears, but it did no good as the next gust tugged them free and put them right back.

Sorcha's heart pounded more erratically with every step she took. She was the last person who should be here. She was a horrible liar. Not only that, but she also caved under pressure. Always. There was a reason she liked her solitude. She didn't have to answer to anyone, and no one looked to her for anything.

Which meant she couldn't let anyone down.

But this was bigger than her. It was bigger than the Skye Druids. That's why she was here. No longer could she turn a blind eye to what was going on. What Usaeil had done to Corann, the leader of the Skye Druids, was enough to convince Sorcha to get off her arse.

It had been no surprise when Sorcha learned that Rhona had taken over as leader of the Druids. As soon as she heard the news, she went to Rhona and offered to do anything to help. It'd never entered her mind that Rhona might send her off on a dangerous mission that could very well get her killed.

Sorcha stopped walking. Her thighs burned from the incline. The sky had grown darker from an incoming storm. She turned and looked back the way she'd come. There hadn't been anyone around, and that's how this had been planned. The only way this would work was if she remained unseen. Even so, she and Rhona had come up with a story in case she *was* stopped.

She drew in a deep breath and zipped up her raincoat. Every fiber of her being wanted to return to Skye and the safety of her cottage. For so long, she had buried her head in the sand and let others handle things. All because she was too scared to actually live.

Bracing herself for whatever was to come, Sorcha began walking again. The climb up to the summit was for skilled climbers only. Spray from the sea coated everything in a fine mist, making the rocks and the grass slippery. She had to watch every step she took. And she wasn't even to the most dangerous part yet.

Climbing such cliffs and mountains had been something Sorcha had grown up doing with her mother and sister. She was an expert, but that didn't mean she liked what was happening. She didn't know these cliffs like she did the ones on Skye.

A crack of lightning followed closely by a boom of thunder made her jump. Loose sediment slipped beneath her feet and caused her to slide. She quickly grabbed hold of an outcropping of rock and a clump of grass to stop herself.

"Bloody hell," she murmured and paused long enough to gather herself.

Then she continued. She didn't look back again. Little by little, she progressed over the terrain. She covered a lot of ground before the first raindrop landed on her. Sorcha ignored it as the path became narrower. She glanced up and saw a group of people ahead. The moment she saw them, she ducked down, afraid that they might have seen her, as well.

When no shout of warning or the sound of anyone coming for her followed, Sorcha slowly rose up enough to see ahead. Only then did she continue on. The fat raindrops came down more readily. She lifted up the hood of her raincoat as she inched closer, using the footholds and handholds to keep herself anchored to the cliff. Then —finally—she was there.

Sorcha pressed her forehead to the damp rocks of the cliff and let out a relieved breath. She'd worry about getting back once she was finished here. She strained her ears to listen, but she couldn't make out any of the words being said by the group. She had come this far. There was no way she would leave without something.

She reached up and grabbed a rock before she set her foot on another and climbed. It was only a meter's difference, but it allowed her to hear. The only problem was that she needed to hang off the side of the cliff to do it.

"…you have to see," a woman said, her Irish accent thick. "Now is our time. We can no longer stand back and wait for someone to come to us. It's time *we* act."

A man snorted loudly. "We might be Druids, but we do not

stand a chance against the Fae. I've heard they're gathering their own group."

"Fek the Fae," the woman stated angrily. "This isn't their world. It's ours!"

A cheer went up from the others.

"You say that until a Fae shows up," the man retorted. "I doubt you'd be so quick to say those words if they did."

Sorcha raised up enough to try and see who had spoken. The crowd stood in a circle. A glow emanated from the ground in the center of the group, the light showing everyone's face, including the man and woman in the middle. The woman was in her mid-forties with chin-length straight, black hair laced with gray. She was attractive with a trim figure she showed off with tight-fitting clothes.

The man appeared his forties, as well. He was tall with broad shoulders and a beer belly that looked as if he'd sported it for many years. His blond hair had thinned on the top, and the comb-over he seemed to prefer, blew in the wind.

Sorcha knew that the Fae sometimes liked to use glamour to disguise their beauty so they could walk among mortals. There was always a chance there could be Fae around, but she didn't think the two main speakers were it. The fact that she was hiding proved just how secretive this meeting was. And how secure the area had been.

None of them seemed concerned with the cliffs, because only someone highly skilled—or an idiot—would even dare what she was doing.

Sorcha was pretty sure she was also an idiot, but there was no turning back now. She was here, and she would finish her mission so she could return with intel for the Druids. Then, she would go back to her cottage and return to the hermit lifestyle she'd lived for the past decade.

The woman in the middle of the circle shook her head. "Patrick, isn't it time we stood up to the Fae? Isn't it time we showed everyone who we are?"

"We?" Patrick asked with a bark of laughter. "You can combine all of our magic together, and it still wouldn't be enough against *one* Fae. How the bloody hell do you think we can fight against them?"

"Who said anything about fighting them?" she asked with a pointed look.

Patrick ran a hand down his face and walked away a few steps before turning back to her. "You've lost your mind. You're basing all of this on hearsay."

"Hearsay from someone who is a Fae," she pointed out.

"Beth, that Fae could've been planted at the pub so you'd overhear him and do all of this."

"You heard him, too."

Patrick sighed as he dropped his chin to his chest and put his hands on his hips. After a few tense moments where the only sound was the rain pelting the ground, he lifted his head. "The Others were disbanded. Whatever their main goal was, we'll never know. But what we do know is that they're gone."

"There's no way they're gone," Beth said.

There were nods of agreement from the other Druids around the circle, some adding "ayes," as well.

Sorcha's arms started to ache. She wasn't sure how much longer she could stay in this position.

"It was probably all a lie," Patrick said.

A woman with dark skin stepped forward. "It isn't a lie. I can say that because I was part of the Others. Moreann chose me herself."

Everyone looked at the woman, including Sorcha. She memorized the woman's features, all while hoping to hear a name.

Beth gave Patrick an I-told-you-so expression. "Between her words and what we overheard, I decided to call this rally together with those I knew were not only powerful enough to stand against the Fae but also strong enough mentally to know what they're getting into."

Patrick ignored Beth and looked at the other woman. "Where is Moreann?"

"I don't know. I've not heard from her in weeks."

Patrick threw up his hands and glared at Beth. "See?"

"But…" the woman said, drawing out the word to get everyone's attention. "I can tell you that I was visited by the Dragon

Kings, who made it very clear that I was to forget anything to do with the Others."

At the mention of the Dragon Kings, some Druids stepped back, visibly shaken, while others frowned in concern. Sorcha knew of the Kings, but she had never met one. She honestly wasn't sure she wanted to. She knew they protected this realm and had since the beginning of time, but they were obviously a group that one simply didn't want to fuck with on any level.

Beth jerked her head to the woman. "Dragon Kings? You never said anything about them."

"Why does it matter?" the woman asked with a twist of her lips.

"It matters because of who they are," Patrick told her. "You should take their warning to heart."

The woman laughed. "The Others were out to destroy the Kings. And it was working, too."

Patrick rolled his eyes. "Obviously not if the Others are gone, and the Kings are still here. And why would the Others want to be rid of the Kings?"

"None of that matters!" Beth shouted and slashed her arm through the air to halt any more talk. "We're here because the Others needed Druids. That's what we are. If the Fae think they can form a group themselves to take over what the Others began, then there's no reason we can't do the same."

This time, it was Sorcha who rolled her eyes. She debated showing herself to the group to tell them the facts of what had happened between the Others, the Dragon Kings, the Fae, and the Druids. Still, she realized none of them would believe her. They wanted their own version of the facts, and that was the only thing they would listen to. It would be her folly if she allowed them to know that she was here.

No longer able to hold herself up, she let her arms straighten so she could lower herself down. It didn't take long for her to realize that the words of the group were garbled once more. Sorcha steeled herself and resumed the position to pull herself up.

"We need to take a vote," Patrick said.

Beth nodded and folded her arms over her chest. "I agree. All for creating a Druid group, raise your hand."

Sorcha's gaze scanned the circle to see that more than half had raised their hands.

"Against?" Patrick asked as he raised his.

Fewer people were completely against the idea, but even more in the circle hadn't chosen a side at all.

Beth flashed a bright smile. "Guess we know who wins."

"Not so quick," Patrick pointed out. "Many didn't vote."

Beth wasn't happy to hear that. She must have realized that if she pushed things now, those who didn't vote might not side with her, which meant that Patrick would have won. Instead, the Druid said, "All right. Let's take a few days to think about it. Let's meet back here again in three days. Everyone who comes must vote. Understood?"

The group nodded and began to turn and hurry away as lightning lit up the sky. With that cue, the rain intensified. Sorcha wanted to stay and listen, see if anything else was exchanged. But between her arms aching and the roar of the rain, she doubted she'd be able to hear anything. Deciding to be safe, she carefully lowered herself and looked over her shoulder at the storm that raged behind her.

She then looked at the cliffside and the narrow trail she'd used. The growing darkness, along with the storm, made it difficult to see. She didn't want to get caught out on the cliffs. It was either go up and climb over the edge with the possibility of someone in the group seeing her. Or she could go back the way she'd come.

Sorcha debated the choices for a moment and decided to chance going back along the cliffs. This wouldn't be the first time she'd gotten caught in a rainstorm while climbing. But it was the first time in Ireland on cliffs she didn't know. And, she was alone. Without anchors.

"Well, this night just keeps getting better and better," she said.

She took a step and was suddenly slammed against the cliffs by a fierce wind gust. Her hands clenched the rock in an effort to stay rooted to the spot. Maybe she should've chanced climbing up and over. Then she thought about being caught climbing up with wind like that, and it sent a chill down her spine.

"Slow and steady," she told herself. The same words her mother had used often with her and her sister.

The rain pelted her now. The droplets were large and heavy as they slammed against her. The lightning, wind, and thunder sounded and felt as if it were on top of her, but she didn't look up to find out. She didn't take her eyes from her route, because all it would take was one slip for her to fall. No one would hear her screams over the storm, and her body would likely not be found for days.

She had no identification on her, so the authorities wouldn't even be able to return her to Scotland. The last thing she wanted was to die in Ireland. She still couldn't believe she was on the isle the Fae called home. She'd hated it for as long as she could remember, and the current situation didn't make her feel all warm and fuzzy.

An eternity later—with a couple of heart-stopping slips—she finally made it back to solid ground. Even then, she had to traverse the rocky terrain down to where she'd parked the rental car.

Sorcha picked up the pace. Now that she was off the cliffside, she felt she could move more quickly. It was a mistake. Within minutes, her foot slipped off a wet rock, and she twisted her ankle. She crumpled, grabbing her injury.

"Dammit," she said as her ankle began to throb.

Out of the corner of her eye, she spotted lightning not far from her. It hit the ground, causing a loud crack. Sorcha screamed and jumped. She had to get to the car and out of the storm. She wasn't safe here. But when she tried to put weight on her injured foot, her eyes welled up with tears.

She fell back onto her butt and slapped her hand on the ground beside her. How could this be happening? She knew better than to rush through terrain she didn't know, but to do it at twilight during a storm? It was a rookie mistake that she shouldn't have made.

Lightning flashed again, revealing the outline of a man about twenty meters below her. He stood as still as a statue as he faced her.

She jumped for a second time, unsure what to do. Was it one of the men from the rally? Someone else?

The man moved slowly toward her before he stopped again. Another flash of lightning revealed his very tall silhouette and incredibly broad shoulders and thick arms showcased by his wet tee shirt that was now molded to his body. She couldn't see much of his face other than a strong jawline and penetrating eyes.

"You seem to be in need of assistance," he said.

She heard the Irish accent in his deep voice. He purposefully kept his distance so as not to scare her. The next flash of lightning had him looking up at the storm above them.

"I think we'd best get out of this weather, don't you?" he asked as he offered her his hand.

There was no way she could get down to her car without help. She had no choice but to trust him. "Yes," she said and took his proffered palm.

He easily lifted her into his arms, cradling her against him. Sorcha felt the movement of his muscles beneath her hands as she wrapped them around his neck. There was no denying the hard stomach against her. Or the softness of the long hair he had gathered at the back of his neck.

There was something about a man with long hair that just did it for her. Few could really pull it off, but she gave credit to those who tried.

Within moments, they were at the bottom of the mountain not far from where she'd hidden her car. She glanced back at the rugged terrain, trying to figure out how he'd come down it so quickly. Had she been so wrapped up in all the hard sinew against her that she hadn't paid attention? There was no other explanation.

"Where shall I take you?"

Her head snapped toward his. That's when she realized that she was very near his face. Unfortunately, she still couldn't get a good look at him. "Oh. Um…my car is parked over there," she said, pointing in the general direction.

He said nothing else as he strode to her vehicle. Once there, he gently set her down until she leaned against the car with her injured foot lifted.

"Thank you," she said.

He gave a nod. "You should be careful. These are dangerous times, and there are many more dangers out there."

She couldn't tell if he was threatening her or warning her, not that it mattered. She was well aware of what was out there. Sorcha pulled the key fob from her pants' pocket and unlocked the vehicle. "You're very right." She opened the car door. "Thank you a—"

But when she glanced up, he was gone. Sorcha didn't look for him. Instead, she got into the car and locked the doors before starting the engine.

CHAPTER TWO

Cathal hadn't moved from his spot near the Halfling, but he was veiled. Which meant that no one but another Reaper—or Death herself—could see him. The last thing he'd expected to see that night was a Halfling on the cliffs listening to a bunch of Druids talk about creating an offshoot group of Others.

After everything the Dragon Kings had gone through to end the Others, it boggled his mind that Druids and Fae now wanted to create their own groups. The only difference was, the Druids didn't stand a chance.

Cathal watched as the car carrying the Halfling drove away. There had been no mistaking her Scottish accent. That only added to his confusion as to why she had been out here tonight. And not just for a walk. She had scaled the side of the cliff to listen to the Druids.

He'd kept one eye on the assembled group, and another on her in case she fell. But the Halfling had been more than competent—even in the storm. Everything would've been fine had she been more careful on her way down the mountain. She had been in too much of a hurry, though, and it'd caused her to hurt an ankle.

Before he knew it, he'd lowered his veil and spoken with her. He still wasn't sure what had come over him. Maybe it was because there had been no one else to help her—and she'd definitely needed assistance. No matter how curious he was to know her intentions, he hadn't asked. She wouldn't have told him anything anyway.

The air shifted slightly, and Rordan appeared beside him. He was smiling, which made Cathal roll his eyes.

"You didn't think I'd see you helping the Halfling, did you?" Rordan asked cheerfully.

Cathal shot him a flat look. "Wipe that smile off your face before I do it for you."

In the next instant, Aisling joined them. "Listen to him, Rordan," she advised.

"You two are no fun," Rordan replied with a frown.

Aisling cut her eyes to Cathal and simply stared. She had red eyes, just as he did, marking them both as Dark Fae. Or at least they *had been* Dark at one time. Being a Reaper meant that whatever happened before you died, no longer mattered once you were reborn to serve Death.

"Why did you help her? She's a Halfling. She would've been just fine on her own," Aisling said.

Cathal felt the gaze of both Reapers on him. He shrugged. "I… don't know."

"It's not like you're going to see her again, so it doesn't matter."

Rordan smiled as he crossed his arms over his chest. "He helped the Halfling because he likes her."

It took a great deal of effort not to punch Rordan, but Cathal managed to keep his hands to himself. Rordan's comments were rarely directed at him. Clearly, he wasn't so lucky this night.

"What?" Rordan said with a chuckle as Aisling speared him with a flat look. "When have you ever seen Cathal help a Halfling? Like I'm just supposed to let that go without comment?" He rolled his silver eyes. "Puh-lease."

Aisling shook her head of long, black and silver braids but didn't reply.

Cathal watched until the car's taillights were out of view. The Halfling had been wary of him, which was smart. The fact that she'd been there secretly intrigued him. He'd wanted to ask her what she was about, but she would've likely made up some lie. And he couldn't stand to hear that, no matter the reason.

Regardless of how he looked at it, he couldn't figure out why a Halfling was there. Unless she was spying on someone in the group. That made him pause. She didn't appear as if she were following a specific person. In fact, she'd seemed intrigued by everyone and everything. That brought him back to why she had been on the mountain to begin with.

A Scotswoman, at that.

Rordan said, "Looks like we have a lot to report. Shall we head back?"

"You two go ahead," Cathal said. "I've got something to do first." The moment the words were out of his mouth, Cathal knew Rordan would comment on them. He pointed a finger at his friend and shook his head. "Not a word. Not one single bloody word."

Rordan slapped his hands against his thighs. "You're no fun. No fun at all."

"I know that look," Aisling told Cathal. "You're going to follow the Halfling. Why?"

He shrugged. "Something doesn't add up with her being here."

"What does it matter what a Halfling does?" Aisling said dismissively.

"Unless the Fae Others recruited her and sent her," Rordan stated.

Cathal hadn't thought of that. He ran a hand down his face,

wiping away the rain. None of them cared about the storm. "She was nervous."

"I would be as well out in a storm like this on a cliff." Aisling shrugged. "Then again, I wouldn't have been that stupid to get into such a predicament."

Rordan twisted his lips. "Unless she had no choice."

Damn. The more they spoke, the more Cathal had to know what was going on with the Halfling. He wanted to let it go. He wished he could. But he couldn't. Something about her affected him. Maybe it was the fact that she didn't appear to know she was a Halfling. It could be because she had been soaked, scared, and entirely at the mercy of the elements. Perhaps it was because she'd put on a brave face, even though he'd seen her vulnerability despite it.

Aisling sighed loudly. "Fine. Let's go after her."

"What?" Cathal asked in surprise as he looked at both of them. "No. There's no need. I'll go alone."

Rordan slapped him on the back. "Sorry, big guy. Death sent us here together. We're going to return together. If that means we take a little detour, then we go as a team."

"He's right," Aisling said before Cathal could speak.

Cathal knew better than to argue with them. Neither would relent. It was better to just agree and allow them to accompany him. The quicker he figured out what the Halfling was doing, the sooner they could return to Death and relay what the Druids were planning.

As if the Reapers didn't have enough shite to deal with. First, the Fae forming their own group, and now the Druids. What was wrong with everyone? The Dragon Kings had annihilated the Others, and the Others were the only ones who had a fighting chance of actually killing the Kings. There was no way any random group of Fae or Druids would even come close to doing harm to the Dragon Kings.

Unless they weren't after the Kings.

"If that frown gets any deeper, we can call it the Grand Canyon," Rordan said.

Cathal glanced at him to find the Reaper's silver eyes on him. He blinked. "What?"

"You're frowning," Aisling told him. "And it's a whopper."

Cathal released a long breath. "I don't like what I'm thinking."

"Let's ease all of our minds and find the Halfling. I'm not at all happy that she was here." Aisling raised her black brows. "And I heard her. She's Scottish."

"Fek me. Really?" Rordan asked in disbelief.

Cathal didn't say another word as he focused on thoughts of the Halfling. He remained veiled and teleported to the next village to see if she'd arrived. This was the closest town to the meeting place of the Druids, but there were three others she could've gone to.

"It's too close," Aisling said as she and Rordan appeared next to Cathal. "She was there to spy. No way would she dare to stay here and take the chance of someone spotting her or her vehicle."

Rordan's silver eyes were narrowed as he scanned the streets. "Two of the Druids from the meeting are here."

"There are three other villages. Let's split up and look for her," Cathal told them.

Aisling nodded. "I'll check Moyarget."

"I've got Ballyvoy," Rordan said.

In the next blink, they were gone. Cathal then teleported to Capecastle. Within seconds of his arrival, he spotted the Halfling's vehicle heading through the village. She parked in front of a bed and breakfast and got out to limp to the door. He remained outside, watching the building.

His gaze moved to a window that lit up from within. He couldn't see movement inside the room, but he had a suspicion that it was the Halfling. As he thought of ways to get inside the B&B, the front door opened, and the Halfling limped out, now wearing dry clothes.

Cathal debated whether to approach her, but as he saw her gaze scanning the streets, he thought better of it. Instead, he remained veiled and walked a few paces behind her. If someone were after her, they wouldn't get past him. Not until he had his answers, at least.

The storm was headed toward them, but the Halfling didn't

seem to care. She took her time getting to the pub because of her injured ankle. Once inside the establishment, she went to a back corner and slid into a booth. At that moment, Rordan and Aisling appeared beside him, both veiled. They waited until some people walking near them had passed before they spoke.

"I would've chosen this village, as well," Aisling said. "She's smart."

Rordan watched her. "I've seen my fair share of Halflings. Some know their ancestry, and others don't. I can't tell which side she falls on."

Neither could Cathal. Maybe that's what intrigued him. It couldn't be her oval face, high cheekbones, full lips, emerald green eyes, or her auburn hair. It certainly wasn't her soft body that he'd held in his arms.

He swallowed and found his friends looking at him. "What?"

"Oh, you like her," Rordan said with a grin.

Aisling's red lips curved into a smile. "I'm in agreement with Rordan. I think you've got the hots for the Halfling."

Cathal shrugged away their words. It wouldn't do any good to dissuade them from their thoughts, so he didn't bother. "I'm going to talk to her."

"Whoa. Hold up there, big guy," Rordan said. "I don't think that's a good idea. She'll find it suspicious if you suddenly show up here after helping her out."

Aisling wrinkled her nose. "He's right."

"Standing out here isn't doing any good," Cathal stated, not bothering to hide his irritation.

Aisling stared at the Halfling through the pub windows. "It doesn't take a lot to notice that she's on edge and guarded. If there's any chance of us getting information from her, it won't be tonight."

"Then when?" Cathal asked.

Rordan glanced at them. "We follow her wherever she goes. That'll give us answers."

Before Cathal could say how much he didn't like that response, Aisling said, "That's too much time. I agree with Cathal.

Something's not quite right here, but the others are waiting on us to return and give a report on what we found tonight."

"She's part of it," Cathal said.

"Probably, but that's for Death to decide," Aisling told him.

He knew it. Though he wanted to stay and talk to the Halfling, that wasn't going to happen. "Let's go."

The three teleported to the small isle in the middle of a loch in Scotland where a hidden Fae doorway stood. They stepped through it and onto Death's realm. It had only recently been opened to the Reapers, and it was nice to have a place to call home once more.

Cathal should feel good now that Usaeil was officially dead, and the Others were no more, but he couldn't quite manage it. Not when there were other groups ready and willing to join together for a similar cause. If it hadn't been for Dubhan and Kyra, Cathal wouldn't have discovered just how many Fae had been vying to get into the Others.

That group was now on Death's and the Reapers' radar—and Cathal had a bad feeling about them. On top of all of that, they still hadn't found Xaneth. The longer the Light Fae remained missing, the more Cathal feared he was dead.

Following Aisling and Rordan, Cathal barely paid any attention to the numerous plants and animals that inhabited the area around the entrance to the realm. He looked up to the white tower that rose above everything. It was Death's home. But Erith no longer resided there alone. She and Cael were now mated. They were a good team, their love making them even stronger together.

Cael had once led the first group of Reapers. He'd been powerful in his own right, but when all the Reapers went up against an old enemy of Erith's, Cael had been caught in the crossfire. Instead of dying, Cael actually acquired additional powers. In fact, he was now a god. Fitting since Death was a goddess.

The moment the three of them walked into the tower, Death appeared with Cael by her side. Erith's long, blue-black hair was pulled over one shoulder, and her lavender eyes were locked on Cathal. He wasn't surprised. There were few things she *didn't* know.

"Well?" Cael asked them.

Cathal remained silent as Aisling and Rordan gave the detailed report of everything that had happened, including him talking to the Halfling. Not once did Erith's gaze leave his.

"And?" Death asked.

Cathal shrugged. "I have nothing to add."

Erith quirked a black brow. "You followed her because you had a gut feeling."

"I did. Something wasn't right. It was as Aisling and Rordan said. She's Scottish and a Halfling. And she was there to spy. I thought it odd and wanted to know who she was spying for."

Cael crossed his arms over his chest. "I would've done the same."

"Me, as well," Eoghan said as he walked into the tower.

Cathal turned his head to the leader of their group of Reapers. Eoghan had been one of the original Reapers before he was promoted to lead his own group and found a way to unite those under him. Each group had seven Reapers, including the leader. They were a ragtag bunch with issues a mile-long. It spoke to Eoghan's strength of will and determination that he had found a way to reach each of them so they worked as a fluid team.

"There's something about the Halfling," Aisling said into the silence. "I can't pinpoint it, but she's different. Aloof and cautious."

Erith nodded as she looked at Aisling. "Like someone who is used to spying?"

"Like someone who is doing it because they must," Cathal replied.

Aisling glanced at him before she nodded. "Exactly."

"I second both of them," Rordan said.

Eoghan considered that for a moment. His quicksilver eyes studied each of them. "Do you think she knows she's a Halfling?"

"Debatable," Rordan answered. "None of us could decide one way or another."

Death drew in a breath and released it. "Only one way to find out."

Cathal held his breath, hoping that Erith would send him after the Halfling. He didn't understand his need to go, only knew that he had to. And if he weren't sent, he'd find a way to go anyway.

"Aisling, you and Cathal will find the Halfling. If she's working with the Fae, I want to know," Erith ordered.

Cathal released a breath and tried not to let it show that he was pleased with his new mission. But he was ready to go now. Waiting around made him anxious, something he wasn't used to feeling. He shifted uncomfortably, noting how Eoghan watched him closely.

"And me?" Rordan asked.

Erith's gaze dropped to the floor for a heartbeat. "You will join the other Reapers in looking for Xaneth."

"You know how to look for the Halfling," Cael told them.

Cathal nodded, holding Cael's purple gaze before he bowed his head to Erith and then looked at Eoghan.

"Come," Eoghan told the three Reapers.

Aisling and Rordan walked together while Cathal found himself alongside Eoghan. Eoghan had not spoken for thousands of years. He only began talking again right before he became leader of their group. Even now, he was a man of few words. Normally, it was something Cathal appreciated, but not so much today.

Once the four of them were outside the tower, Eoghan stopped. They looked at him, waiting for whatever it was he had to say. He didn't make them wait for long.

"If the Halfling is working with the Fae, she'll have to be stopped."

Aisling gave a nod.

Cathal wasn't so quick to agree. "Any Fae? Or the ones who are trying to fill the role of the Others?"

"The ones you and Dubhan ran into not so long ago," Eoghan said, a slight grin on his lips.

Aisling flicked back her long hair in its many small braids. "I can't imagine those Fae would bring in a Halfling."

"One that's Scottish?" Rordan said with a shrug. "What if there's a connection between her and the Dragon Kings?"

Cathal snorted. "No Fae would be that stupid."

"We don't know anything," Eoghan said, interrupting them.

"This is the time for us to gather information. Any of it. All of it. I don't care how small you think it is, we need to know. That group of Fae could disrupt things."

Eoghan referred to how the infamous Light Fae, Rhi—daughter to the now-deceased ex-Queen of the Light, and newly mated to the King of Dragon Kings, Constantine—were trying to unite the two factions of Fae under one council with the help of a Dark Fae named Noreen. Things weren't going exactly to plan. Some Fae were completely against it.

The Others had remained hidden for a long time. At least they had been hidden from the Reapers and Dragon Kings. Apparently, they had been recruiting both Fae and Druids behind the scenes to get the most powerful of both to join. The Others, however, had only been comprised of six people. A Dark and Light Fae, a *mie* and *drough* Druid from this planet, and a *mie* and *drough* Druid from another realm where the humans had originated. The combination of the magic of those six individuals was powerful enough to go against the Dragon Kings. Before the Others, nothing and no one had magic more powerful than the Kings.

That's what shocked Cathal. Because no matter how powerful the Fae were, no matter how many of them joined forces, it wouldn't be enough to take down the Dragon Kings.

If that was even their end goal.

CHAPTER THREE

It was good to be home. Sorcha was never happier than when she arrived back on the Isle of Skye. She wanted to go straight to her house, but instead, she went to see Rhona since she knew her cousin would want a report immediately. Sorcha hadn't slept at all the night before. And not just because of climbing after not doing it for so long or because she had been spying. No, it was mostly because of the man who had helped her. She couldn't stop thinking about him.

An hour before dawn, she'd left the B&B and turned in the rental car before climbing back into her trusty ancient Range Rover and driving onto the ferry that would start her return trip to

Scotland. All the while, she looked around, hoping that no one followed her. She was new to the spy business, and she wasn't sure if she could even get herself out of a jamb. Her goal was to make sure she didn't find herself in one.

It took over nine hours from the time she left Ireland until she arrived home. She was exhausted both mentally and physically. She hoped that what she had done was enough for Rhona because Sorcha wasn't sure she could survive another night like the one she'd just had. All she wanted was to climb into her bed and sleep for the next few days. Yet she rubbed her tired eyes and stifled a yawn after she pulled up in front of her cousin's house, knowing that wouldn't happen quite yet.

Rhona's bright green eyes held a smile when she opened the front door. "Good to have you home, cousin."

"It's good to be back. You were right, by the way."

Rhona's smile slipped, unease filling her gaze. "I'd hoped I wasn't. Come inside."

The two went in, where tea waited in the back room. Neither spoke until they had a cup in hand and were sitting comfortably on a sofa. Sorcha was having a hard time keeping her eyes open. Now that she was back, the weariness was settling in.

"Perhaps you'd better get started," Rhona said.

Sorcha set aside her cup and began relaying everything that had happened, including the man who'd carried her to the car.

"How is your ankle?"

Sorcha shrugged. It hurt like hell, but as soon as she was able to get it elevated, it should be all right. "It'll be fine."

"Was he one of the Druids?" Rhona asked.

Sorcha shook her head. "I couldn't see all their faces, but I don't believe so. He didn't ask me anything."

"That's not always a good sign. He might have seen you spying on them."

"I wasn't followed. I made sure of that."

Rhona's lips flattened for a moment. "Did you use magic like I told you to?"

This was the only thing that was a point of contention between them. Sorcha was a Druid, but magic had made her lose all that she held dear. Because of that, she chose not to use it at all anymore. It was a part of her life that she had given up freely and willingly, even while most of the other Druids on Skye couldn't understand her reasoning.

"Sorcha," Rhona admonished. "That's how you keep yourself safe."

"I was fine without it."

"I think you were lucky." Rhona released a long sigh. "You're our best climber. You're also one with powerful magic. That's why I sent you."

Sorcha lowered her gaze to the floor. "You know why I won't use magic."

"You're back, and you got us great intel. Thank you. You've done more than I could've hoped. I've kept you long enough. You need rest."

Actually, she'd done exactly what Rhona had asked for, but Sorcha didn't mention that. She forced a smile and got to her feet. "What does all of this mean for us on Skye?"

"I don't know yet. Makes me wish Corann was still alive," Rhona said, sadness filling her eyes.

Sorcha had to agree. Corann had led the Skye Druids for what felt like eternity. He'd been wise and fair, and he'd always known what to do. "You'll do fine. You were Corann's choice to succeed him, and he always made the right decisions."

"I'm utterly out of my depth," Rhona admitted, her face showing her exhaustion.

Sorcha touched her cousin's arm and gave her a comforting smile before she started for the door. She was nearly there when Rhona's voice reached her.

"Thank you, Sorcha."

She lifted her hand in a wave but didn't turn back. Sorcha slid behind the wheel of her car and sat there for a second, letting everything sink in. Then she started the engine and drove the ten miles to her house.

The moment she walked inside, she felt as if a huge weight had been lifted from her shoulders. She locked the door and limped to her bedroom, where she collapsed onto the bed without removing her clothes. Her eyes closed, and she let herself fall blissfully into sleep.

When Sorcha next opened her eyes, it was to see that the sun had recently risen. She yawned and stretched before she climbed out of bed. She pulled off her clothes and got into the shower, letting the hot water run over her. Her fingers were beginning to prune when she finally turned off the tap and grabbed a towel.

After she dressed, she made her way to the kitchen for some tea. Only then did she head to sit on the front porch and look out at the beauty of Skye. She watched the birds coming to the feeder. The sound of sheep could be heard in the distance. The next field over held Scottish cows, mooing at the sight of their master.

This was home. This was where Sorcha felt safe. She realized now more than ever that there was a reason she hadn't left Skye in years. It had been reaffirmed. Nothing and no one could get her to leave her home again. Ever.

The sound of a vehicle pulling up snagged her attention. She recognized Rhona's car. While it wasn't odd for her cousin to visit, the fact that it came on the heels of her return caused her some concern. Sorcha got to her feet as the vehicle pulled to a stop, and Rhona got out of the car.

"Morning. What brings you here so early?" Sorcha asked with a smile, hoping the knot of worry in her stomach was for naught.

Rhona didn't return the easy expression. Instead, she closed the car door and walked to the porch. She stopped before Sorcha. "News has spread about the meeting of the Druids in Ireland. Some here want us to have the same sort of meeting."

"You aren't, are you?"

"If I don't, someone else will. At least if I arrange it, I can control it."

Sorcha's stomach fell to her feet. "Controlling it and getting the votes you want isn't the same thing."

"What choice do I have?"

"There is always a choice. Corann taught us that."

Rhona looked away, long strands of red hair flying in the breeze. Finally, she slid her gaze back to Sorcha. "If I don't have the meeting, there are so many things that could go wrong."

"When are you planning it?"

"I'm not sure."

"Put it off for as long as you can."

Rhona's brows drew together. "Why?"

"I don't know." And she didn't. It was just something she felt in her gut. "The Druids in Ireland haven't voted yet. That isn't happening for two more days if what I heard is true. Wait for them and see what happens."

"That's a sound idea. I don't suppose I can convince you to go back, can I?"

"Not with my injury." It was a good excuse, and she was glad for it. Sorcha wished she felt better about the talk, but she didn't. Probably because she knew that more was coming. "You didn't come all this way to tell me that, did you?"

"No."

She waited for Rhona to continue, but her cousin remained silent. Finally, Sorcha said, "Spit it out."

"It's time for you to go to the Fairy Pools."

Sorcha took a step back, feeling as if she'd been punched. She winced at the pain in her ankle and quickly shifted her weight to keep it slightly lifted. "I told you I wasn't ever going back."

"It's a family tradition. You can't ignore that."

"I've ignored it for ten years. I figured I could keep doing that."

Rhona blew out a breath. "I told you I'd never make you. Corann never made you. But one day, you're going to have to let go of the past."

"When I die."

"There hasn't been a Fae on Skye since Usaeil took Corann and killed him."

Sorcha shot her a flat look. "That was only a week ago."

"The spells in place will alert us if any Fae do arrive, but we can't keep them out. We're not that powerful."

Sorcha glared at her cousin, trepidation rising quickly. "Why tell me this?"

"In case that's what's keeping you locked in your house."

"I stay here—alone—because that's how I like it."

Rhona shook her head sadly. "We miss you."

"You see me."

"Not like I used to."

Sorcha shrugged. "Unfortunately, that's how it's going to be."

Rhona smiled sadly, then wrapped her arms around Sorcha for a hug. "I love you, cousin. Know that you're the only one who holds onto the past. You're young and beautiful and have so much to give. Please don't keep yourself locked away here."

Before Sorcha could reply, Rhona released her and turned on her heel to walk back to her car. Sorcha watched as the vehicle drove out of sight, Rhona's words ringing in her ears. Sorcha wanted to ignore everything that had been said, but she couldn't.

She limped into the house and went to make some toast. The moment she pulled the bread out, she realized that she had forgotten to send her grocery list to Noah. He picked up anything she needed from town and brought it to her for a small fee. It saved her from having to get out and…socialize. And it made him some money.

It had begun with his older brother, Harry. Once Harry finished his schooling and went off to start his life, Sorcha asked Noah if he'd like to take over the job. Noah had been quick to agree. And, for the past two years, things had been going fine. The only problem was that Noah was about to finish his schooling and leave Skye.

Sorcha found her mobile phone and made a list of items she needed to refill her pantry and fridge before sending it to Noah. She set her phone down and walked away to make her toast. She heard the mobile ding, letting her know that someone had sent a text. No doubt it was Noah letting her know that he'd be by sometime today with the groceries.

She didn't look at her phone until she finished eating her buttered toast. The message was from Noah, but it wasn't to tell her he would bring her items. She blinked at the text, then checked her calendar.

"Shite," she murmured.

How had she forgotten the date Noah was leaving? She knew the answer. She'd been too wrapped up in leaving her home for Ireland and undertaking a dangerous mission to recall those details. Noah had left the same day she had, and she had completely forgotten about it.

Since she didn't readily know anyone who could assume his position, it meant that she would have to suck it up and go into town herself. But that didn't have to be today. She sent a quick text to Noah, apologizing and wishing him well in his new life. Then she grabbed her headphones and went to the sofa to listen to an audiobook. She'd think about dealing with her groceries later.

She soon realized that her head wasn't in the book. She shut it off and removed the headphones. Her mind kept returning to the Fairy Pools. She didn't want to go. No matter what Rhona said, Sorcha didn't need to be there. Yet she couldn't ignore the guilt that pulled at her. And she hated feeling guilty about anything.

Although that was the very reason she had gone to Ireland for her cousin in the first place.

Sorcha rolled her eyes as she dropped her head back on the sofa and stared at the ceiling. The Fairy Pools were a place she had gone to with her family numerous times. And not just for their ritual. Skye drew people to it, those who had even a drop of Druid blood in their veins. But the Fairy Pools were something altogether different. No one who visited could deny the magic that seemed to surround the place.

They had been a particular favorite of Sorcha's. During the summers, she could often be found swimming in one of the many pools, soaking in the sun, and gazing at the glorious mountains surrounding her. Even when it was too cold to swim, she hiked along the pools.

Thinking about it caused memories of her family to fill her mind. She grabbed her head in an effort to stop them, but it was too late. They had already infiltrated. Her mother laughing, her sister teasing her. They had been the Three Musketeers, doing everything together. They were closer than most families could even dream about. Not that they didn't argue. With three women, the fights could get very heated, but they never lasted long.

A tear slipped down Sorcha's face. She hastily dashed it away. Even after a decade, memories of her family could still gut her like nothing else. It was why she didn't think back to those times too often. They might be good memories, but it was also a reminder of what she no longer had.

And what she had done.

Forgiveness wasn't something she could give herself or accept from others. She deserved everything she had gotten. Whatever life she had thought to have had died the day her mother and sister did.

Sorcha blew out a breath and lifted her head. She looked around the small cottage she'd lived in for her entire life. At first, she hadn't changed any of her mother's decorating. But after a while, Sorcha needed to take away things that roused too many memories. Eventually, over the last ten years, the cottage had become distinctly hers. While her mother and sister had loved to collect all sorts of things, Sorcha was more of a minimalist. And that was reflected in everything from the furniture to the clothes she wore.

Her gaze lowered to her ankle. It was still a little swollen, but it wasn't broken. She'd feared that the night of the storm, but she hadn't wanted to think about anything but getting away from the cliffs. The drive home had only made it worse because she hadn't been able to keep it elevated. Sleeping for as long as she had, had helped things, but if she wanted to walk normally again, then she needed to get the swelling down.

You could've asked Rhona to help with it.

The minute the thought went through her head, Sorcha got angry at herself. If she wasn't going to do magic to help herself, she certainly wasn't going to ask someone else to do it for her.

It would be so easy for you to fix the ankle.

It would, but this wasn't the first time she had hurt herself. Nor would it be the last. Magic wasn't meant to be used for such things.

It was a powerful tool, and in the wrong hands, it could do lasting damage. As she well knew.

She shifted so she lay on the sofa. Sorcha used the pillows at the end to stack beneath her ankle to elevate the leg. She didn't bother trying to listen to the audiobook again. Her thoughts were too jumbled for that. Neither could she read. She debated turning on the tele but decided against it.

Instead, she stared at the ceiling, going over everything that had happened in the last few months. The Isle of Skye had been a refuge for Druids. It had also been a stronghold that no one dared to threaten. All that ended with Usaeil. She had once been the Queen of the Light Fae, ruling for thousands upon thousands of years. But it had all been a lie. She had murdered her own family to take the throne. Her entire reign had been a deception since she had used glamour to hide the fact that she was really a Dark Fae.

Things got worse from there. Apparently, Usaeil had begun killing Druids to take their magic and strengthen hers. No doubt she had gotten the idea from the Others—which she had helped to create.

Usaeil had been the one to come to Skye and ask the Druids to guard the Fairy Pools. It gave the Druids a false sense of power that Usaeil had proven when she came to Skye and took two Druids, one of them Corann. Because the Skye Druids had more magic than other Druids, they increased Usaeil's power significantly.

Corann, in his infinite wisdom, had known his role in the game Usaeil and Moreann—the Druid from the other realm—played. Corann had long known that his fate was connected to Moreann's. It was something he'd kept to himself until the end when he'd shared it with Rhona as his spirit passed into the next phase.

The safety the isle always seemed to have was shattered the day Corann was taken. It was a new dawn for those on Skye, but they weren't the only ones. The Dragon Kings, as well as the Warriors and Druids of MacLeod Castle, also faced new times. The Kings had seemed to come out ahead, at least for the moment. As had the Warriors and Druids. Sorcha couldn't say the same for those on Skye.

Everything felt as if they teetered on the edge of a knife. One wrong slip and they could fall into a quagmire of shite so deep, they'd never pull themselves out. And all Rhona could think about was Sorcha going to the ritual at the Fairy Pools.

"No way in hell," Sorcha stated.

CHAPTER FOUR

"Skye?" Aisling stated in shock, and a little bit of annoyance. "You've got to be kidding me."

Cathal was as surprised as she. He was more troubled by why a Halfling would be living on Skye. While mortals without magic lived on the isle, it was a haven for Druids. There were more Druids on Skye than anywhere else in the world.

He and Aisling stood veiled outside a stone cottage. It was perched atop a hill with lovely views in every direction. Reapers could locate Halflings, and he had been drawn to the Isle of Skye whenever he thought about the woman. Unease rippled through him as he wondered why.

"Please tell me you got it wrong," Aisling prodded.

Cathal shrugged and glanced at her. "We won't know until we take a look."

"You go ahead. I'll stay here."

He frowned as he faced her, wondering why she seemed so irritated. Then he realized what it was. "You'd rather be searching for Xaneth."

Aisling released a long breath and met his gaze. "Xaneth helped us. And because of it, Usaeil targeted him. The longer he goes without being found, the more I think he's dead."

"If he was, Death would've felt his soul. She hasn't."

"That doesn't mean Usaeil didn't do something to him."

Cathal couldn't argue with that. Usaeil had done a great many things that no one had seen coming, including casting a spell that kept her returning from the dead, again and again. Rhi, along with Con and the other Dragon Kings, had finally taken care of that. Though the armies of the Light and Dark Fae had also been involved.

Aisling flattened her lips. "Not that this isn't as important—"

"You don't need to say more," he interrupted her. "I understand."

Probably more than she realized.

Aisling shot him a quick smile. "Thanks."

"I'll take a look inside to see if it's the Halfling. Be right back."

Cathal didn't wait for a response as he teleported inside the house. He got in easily, which meant that there were no markings to keep Reapers out. Not that a Druid would know of such spells, but at this point, nothing would surprise him.

He looked around the homey dwelling, noting the simple décor in shades of light gray, white, and cream. It gave the place a contemporary air, except for the dated appliances that only seemed to add to the charm, instead of detracting from it.

Then his gaze landed on the woman reclining on the sofa. Her auburn curls were spread out on the pillow she rested on as her emerald eyes stared at the ceiling. She wore a pair of jeans and a soft beige shirt and had her injured foot resting on a stack of pillows. He couldn't believe that he had found her so quickly.

As soon as that emotion went through him, apprehension returned. What was a Halfling doing living on the Isle of Skye surrounded by Druids? Then he thought of the Fairy Pools. There was a good chance that the Halfling was here for the pools. As easy as that connection was, Cathal didn't buy it.

He might be veiled, but it didn't mean that someone couldn't hear him. All Fae could veil themselves for a few seconds. Only Reapers—and a special few Fae like Rhi—were powerful enough to do it for as long as they wanted.

Cathal couldn't tear his gaze away from the Halfling. She had been pretty in the middle of a storm, drenched and needing help. Now, she was so stunning, she stole his breath. Her creamy skin had a few freckles scattered across her nose and along her chest. Her toenails were painted an iridescent gray with a chip on the inside corner of her left big toe.

She hadn't moved her gaze from the ceiling, and he couldn't help but wonder what it was that she thought about. He wished he could reveal himself and talk to her. That almost made him snort because he wasn't what anyone would call a talker. He much preferred the silence. There was so much a person could notice and pick up on if they only shut their mouths for a few minutes. Unfortunately, few people adhered to such a rule.

Except the Halfling.

Cathal found himself moving closer to her. He noticed that she wore a delicate gold necklace that had a shield knot dangling from the chain—a symbol of protection for the Druids. At the sight of it, his trepidation doubled. In a blink, he returned to Aisling.

The female Reaper stood with her arms crossed over her chest and a foot tapping in annoyance. "Took you long enough. Where are we off to next? I felt a Halfling near Arran."

"It's her."

Aisling's foot stopped mid-tap. Red eyes slid to the cottage before returning to him. "You're sure?"

"Go see for yourself."

She took him up on the offer. A few seconds later, Aisling returned. "Fek me. It is her. Did you see her necklace?"

"Aye."

"She's on Skye, wearing a Druid protection symbol. I don't think there's any denying that she's a Druid."

Cathal hid his grimace. "And a Halfling."

"Bloody hell."

He shrugged, trying to throw off his worry. "It isn't the first time."

"It is for a fekking Skye Druid."

"It explains why she was spying on the Druids in Ireland, though."

Aisling rolled her eyes dramatically. "Yeah. She was doing it for her people here. Shite. I honestly believed that the Halfling we searched for wouldn't be here."

"The Skye Druids are powerful. The fact that she's also a Halfling makes her particularly interesting. I cannot imagine what kind of magic she has."

Aisling blew out a breath and dropped her arms to her sides. "All right, big guy. How do you want to play this? You obviously have some kind of connection to this Halfling, so I'm going to let you take the lead. And do not assume I'm doing that because I'd rather be elsewhere."

If there was one thing he'd learned about Aisling, it was that she was as tough as any male Fae he'd ever known. In most cases, tougher. Each Reaper had been through their own kind of Hell in their previous life. And while they didn't share such things with each other, he had an inkling that Aisling's story was particularly appalling.

But she was loyal to the Reapers. She also had more confidence than anyone he knew. Cathal suspected that it was just an act to hide her scars. They all bore them—both visible and invisible—and he assumed Aisling's might be the worst out of all of the Reapers. The fact that she was stepping back had nothing to do with her being unable to make decisions, and everything to do with the fact that she recognized he was somehow attached to the Halfling.

Cathal wasn't at all happy about that connection, but he couldn't ignore it either. "She doesn't appear to be going anywhere for the moment. Let's split up. See what you can find around the isle."

Aisling twisted her lips. "I think it's a good plan, but we should be careful. After what Usaeil did, Fae won't be welcome here."

"They can't stop any from coming. Besides, we aren't Fae anymore. We're Reapers."

She cocked a brow at him. "That doesn't make things better. No Fae can know about us. That means Halflings, too."

"Some have known about us."

"Do you really want to push that? Now? After everything we've been through?" Aisling asked.

Cathal thought about that for a moment before he shook his head. "You're right. I wouldn't even know what to say to her anyway. I don't even know her name."

"I'll go check around the isle. You stay here. You might find something."

In a blink, Aisling was gone. Cathal didn't immediately return inside the cottage. He couldn't shake the feeling that he was supposed to find the Halfling for some reason. But why? And more importantly, why *him*?

Those weren't answers he was likely to get anytime soon. Cathal wasn't the most patient Fae, but being a Reaper had made him… adjust. This was different, though. He could feel it in his gut. He wasn't sure that he liked whatever it was that kept drawing him to the Halfling. It could only mean bad things.

Cathal could stand it no more. He teleported inside the house, making sure his veil was in place. The Halfling still lay on the sofa. She had such a forlorn look on her face that he nearly asked her what was wrong. He couldn't believe himself. He never got involved in anyone's business, and yet, that's precisely what he was doing now. Or at least what he wanted to do.

He could tell himself that it was because of the new Fae group that had formed and the Reapers' interest in that, but he knew that for the shite it was. He could even say that it was because Death had sent him. The truth was that he would've come no matter what. Even if Erith had told him to stay away.

Cathal narrowed his gaze on the Halfling. He wondered if she had done some kind of spell that had drawn him to her. It felt as if she were pulling on a cord that she had wrapped around him. But no Halfling—or any Fae for that matter—could have that kind of control over a Reaper.

He gave himself a shake and used the opportunity to walk around the cottage. There were three bedrooms and one bath. Two of the rooms held furniture, but they didn't appear to have been used in some time. The third was obviously the Halfling's. The bed was unmade, and a pile of dirty clothes lay near the door. Other than that, the space was in meticulous order, just like the rest of the house.

Since her room was at the back, he was able to rifle through a few things without making any noise. He didn't particularly like going through someone's things like this, but he wasn't given much choice. They knew nothing about the Halfling, other than where she lived and that she might very well be a Druid.

That still took him aback. The Fae had always come to Skye because of the Fairy Pools, but they tended not to mess with any of the Druids who called the isle home. As far as Cathal knew, there was no direct order from either the King of the Dark or the Queen of the Light instructing them to keep their distance. It was more like something all Fae simply knew.

He stilled when he saw her small purse. It would be easy to open it and find the identification that humans carried so he could learn her name. But he didn't. He didn't know why, but he wanted her to tell him.

"What the fek is wrong with me?" he whispered as he turned away and walked from the room.

He halted in the hallway when he saw that she now sat up on the couch. After a moment, she pushed to her feet, wobbling slightly as she tried not to put too much weight on her injured ankle. He wasn't sure why she hadn't used magic to heal it. Whether she used Druid magic or Fae, she could heal herself. Yet, she had chosen not to. The longer he was around the Halfling, the more confused he became.

For the next few hours, the woman moved around very little. She ate lunch, went back to the sofa to lie down, got up again an hour later for some tea, then was back on the couch. She put on headphones and listened to an audiobook for about forty-five minutes before she gave up on that with a loud sigh. Then she was back to staring at the ceiling.

Aisling returned to the cottage, and Cathal went outside to talk to her. He jerked his chin. "Find out anything?"

"That meeting we listened to in Ireland? The Druids are going to have one here."

His brows snapped together. "What?"

"The new head of the Druids, Rhona, doesn't want it, but others are calling for it. Appears she realizes that she needs to hold the meeting—if only to try and dissuade the Druids from wanting to create such a group."

Cathal nodded. "Good for her."

"On another note, there seems to be some kind of ritual at the Fairy Pools taking place soon."

His frown deepened. "Ritual? What for?"

"Something to do with a certain family here. Rhona is part of it. It seems she's trying to get someone to the ritual, who hasn't been for some time. A woman by the name of Sorcha. Their mothers were sisters."

Cathal found himself looking at the house.

"Did you discover the Halfling's name?" Aisling asked.

He shook his head. "No."

"Did you look?"

"I did." He swung his head back to her and met her gaze and raised a brow.

She stared at him for a long minute before she nodded. "Got it. The ritual is supposed to take place in a couple of days."

"I know of nothing that would cause the Druids here to do anything for the Fae."

Aisling rolled her eyes. "They're fekking humans. I don't care if they have magic or not, they do some really stupid shite."

He couldn't stop the smile from pulling at his lips. "You're not wrong."

"I didn't see anything else around the isle. Most notably missing were the Fae."

"Part of me isn't surprised. After what Usaeil did—"

"Most Fae don't even know about that."

Cathal blew out a breath as he nodded. "Do you remember how the Fairy Pools came to be?"

Aisling shook her head of long, black and silver braids. "No. Do you?"

"I don't. There is obviously a connection to the Fae here. There are the Fairy Pools, the Fairy Bridge, Fairy Glen, and Fairy Knoll. Our people played a big part here."

"But for all of that, the Fae don't come here very often."

Cathal shrugged. "That we know of."

"Perhaps it's time we dug into the legends to find the truth."

He grinned at her. "You wouldn't be having fun now, would you?"

She cut her red eyes to him. "If you tell anyone, I'll have to hurt you."

"I wouldn't dare," he said as he held up his hands in front of him.

Aisling's lips softened into a smile. "I'm glad you helped the Halfling. And I'm glad I'm here helping you."

"We'll finish here, then we can both look for Xaneth. He'll be found. I know it."

"I wish I had your confidence."

Cathal didn't bother mentioning that she seemed particularly interested in finding Xaneth. Almost as much as Erith. Then again, he had never understood the minds of women. It was best if he kept his thoughts to himself.

CHAPTER FIVE

The first rays of sunlight came over the horizon, dawning a new day as Sorcha stood on the beach. The wind was soft, the smell of salt heavy in the air. Birds began to call as they left their nests to start the day. Memories of her sister, her mother, and herself standing in this exact spot filled her. Lots of laughter, corny jokes, and many serious discussions had happened on this beach.

This cove was one known only to locals, and it had become theirs. This was the first time Sorcha had been here since her family died. She didn't stop the tears that came. Nor did she halt the memories. They had assaulted her all night. She'd soon realized there was no running from them. She had pushed them aside for as long as she could.

Whether she wanted them or not, they were there, forcing her to relive the good—and the bad—times.

For so many years, she'd told herself that she enjoyed being alone. It was a lie. Sadly, she'd almost begun to believe it. The truth was that she missed her family so much that the ache threatened to swallow her whole. Nothing could be done to bring them back. And while so many had told her that time would dull the grief, they were wrong. It had only grown.

As the sun slowly climbed higher in the sky, she watched the reflection upon the water. The sound of the waves gently rolling onto the shore before ebbing away was soothing. She'd forgotten just how much she loved it.

Sorcha wrapped her arms around herself and closed her eyes as she raised her face to the sky. Somehow, by allowing the memories to fill her, she felt…relieved. Her tears dried, and she took a deep, calming breath. She didn't know why she hadn't done this before.

Actually, that was a lie. She hadn't come to the beach because she hadn't felt worthy. She had a penance to pay, and getting any kind of enjoyment out of life wouldn't allow her to serve that sentence. A part of her felt guilty, but she hastily pushed it aside. There was nothing remorseful about watching a sunrise and thinking about the past.

A smile touched her lips as she thought about her mother and her mantras. One of her favorites had been: *Never let anyone make you feel guilty.*

She wondered what her mum would think about her making herself feel remorseful now. But then Sorcha knew what she would say.

"The only one who can make you happy is yourself, Sorcha. You know right from wrong. Follow that and follow your heart. You can't go wrong in doing those two things."

Her face crumpled as fresh tears flowed. God, how she missed her mum. By not allowing herself to delve into the past, she had shut out the words of wisdom her mother had so often shared throughout the years. It felt good—right, even—to hear her mother's voice in her head, repeating the words she had thought so important to share with her daughters.

Sorcha opened her eyes and wiped the tears away. She watched the birds for a little while longer before she turned and slowly picked her way through the rocks to her car. Her ankle was better, but not well enough to be walking on it for too long. Yet that hadn't kept her at home. She'd needed to come to the beach. It soothed her soul in ways she hadn't been able to fathom.

Maybe, subconsciously, she had known what would happen, and that's why she'd come this morning. Whatever the reason, Sorcha was glad she'd made the trip.

She started the engine and backed the vehicle up to turn around. As she stopped to check to make sure no one was coming before she pulled out onto the road, she paused, her thoughts going to Rhona's visit the day before. Sorcha couldn't do the ritual. But… now might be a good time to go to the Fairy Pools. It was still early. Few tourists would be there. It would allow her some time to be alone before she returned to the cottage.

With her decision made, Sorcha pulled out onto the road and headed to the pools. The entire way there, she kept wondering if she should go home. What would she accomplish by going to the pools? Nothing. She refused to attend the ritual, so going now would be silly.

And yet, she kept driving.

"What is wrong with me?" she asked herself.

But she knew. She missed her family, and it had taken its toll. Leaving Skye for Ireland had wound her up tight with anxiety and fear. Coming home should have alleviated all of that. Instead, she was doing things she hadn't done in years.

She slowed and turned onto a narrow road that wound through the countryside. Signs told tourists where to go for the Fairy Pools, but she didn't need them. Sorcha could get there with her eyes closed. The earliest memory she had was of being at the pools with her mum and her sister.

Sorcha pulled into the gravel carpark and shut off the engine.

There wasn't another vehicle in sight. She got out before she changed her mind. The idea had been to only stand at her car, but the next thing she knew, she'd shut the door and walked toward the path that led to the pools. From where she stood, she couldn't see the pools themselves. It looked like gently rolling hills with the Black Cuillin Mountains rising in the distance. The range held the River Brittle, which fed into the pools. It wasn't until you got closer that you realized the water had cut into the ground, and the pools were sunken.

A sign read: *Glumagan Na Sithichean,* with *Fairy Pools* written in English below it. It was a twenty-minute walk from here to the first pool. Sorcha crossed the public road to the start of the path. She paused beside the small green sign labeled *Sligaghan,* Gaelic for *start.*

She felt the draw of the pools just as she used to, just as every Druid did. But she hesitated. She glanced down at her ankle, thankful that she had put on a brace that morning. There was a good chance she could hurt herself on this trek because it was steep and rough for the first few meters.

Even though a part of her warned that she shouldn't, Sorcha found herself continuing on. About fifty meters from the road, the path split. She had taken both ways multiple times, but her favorite was the right-hand option. She was careful about how she placed her injured foot so as not to aggravate the ankle. The trek went downhill, and it wasn't long before she reached the first river crossing. There, she used the large stepping-stones to cross the water and get onto the gravel path.

From there, the terrain leveled as she walked beside the river. So many times, she and her sister had run this section to see who was fastest. It was one of her favorite spots because it crossed a peat moor with heather. Just ahead, she spotted the large, impressive boulders left after the ice had melted away during the last Ice Age. As the path gently rose, it met up with the main river. Her heart raced as she crossed the second part of the body of water and saw the rough rock steps naturally made by the rapids. Then, the first waterfall came into view.

She paused and took it in. This was the start of the magical pools. This waterfall was the highest with the water tumbling into the deepest pool. And it was a glorious sight to behold. However, it was the next pool that was the most famous because of its beautiful clear blue water. It featured a natural arch, which she had swum beneath numerous times. It was exhilarating and breathtaking.

Every waterfall, every pool, every stone.

There wasn't a place here that didn't conjure a memory of the past for Sorcha. All of them were good, causing her to smile and her eyes to water with unshed tears. This was the first time she had been alone at the pools since her family's deaths, and it was just what she needed.

Sorcha walked to an outcropping of rock near the waterfall. She had jumped off it several times, but this time, she just wanted to sit and take it all in. With her feet dangling over the edge, she closed her eyes and listened to the sound of the water moving past her to fall below. It drowned out any other sound.

For the first time in…ages…she let herself feel the magic that flowed through the pools. She didn't know if it came up from the ground, from the mountains, or if it was the water. Not that it mattered. It was a special place for Druids.

Those on Skye had many rituals that began when a Druid turned twelve and was accepted into the assembly. It was a grand event that took place at the Fairy Pools. Other sacred rituals for Imbolc, the Spring Equinox, Beltane, the Summer Solstice, Lughnasadh, the Fall Equinox, Samhuinn, and finally, the Winter Solstice were held in other locations around Skye. The pools were also a place many Druids chose to be married.

Sorcha had dreamed of her wedding taking place at the pools. She hadn't wanted anything grand, just lots of flowers and her family. Late July or August had been her preference since the heather would be blooming, and the purple flowers along the pools were spectacular.

What an incredible place the pools were. The sheer beauty of them, the land, the mountains, was enough to make anyone feel as if they had finally come home.

"Well, well, well," said a deep voice tinged with an Irish accent behind her. "I didn't expect to see anything more beautiful than the pools here. Then, I spotted you."

Sorcha stiffened at the poor use of a pick-up line. She wasn't in the mood for company. Not to mention, anything even remotely Irish raised her hackles. Without turning around, she said, "I want to be alone."

"Ah, don't do that to me. I could show you a good time."

He'd come closer. She could feel him just a little behind her. If her legs weren't dangling over a boulder next to a waterfall, she would've gotten up and left. But he had boxed her in. And he knew it.

Asshole.

She'd told him how she felt. Her next best option was to ignore him. Hopefully, he'd take the hint. But most guys weren't that clever.

"It's not nice to keep your back turned when someone is speaking with you," he said, a hint of annoyance coloring his words.

Sorcha took a breath to keep her cool. "I appreciate your interest, but as I told you, I wish to be alone."

To her shock, he sat down beside her. She jerked her head to him and saw his silver eyes, black hair, and stunningly gorgeous face and body. A Fae. Of course. It was just her luck that one of the assholes had chosen today to come to the pools. She really hoped Rhona and the other Druids had been alerted that a Fae was on Skye. It made her wonder why she hadn't felt the spells signaling her. Then again, she hadn't used magic in a decade. Perhaps this was the magic's way of getting back at her.

He smiled. Most women would probably fall all over themselves to get his attention. But she wasn't most women. Sorcha looked away, trying to figure out how she could jump up and get away without hurting her ankle or falling into the water.

"Not even a smile?" he said with a shake of his head. "You could at least ask my name."

Sorcha had had enough. She bit back a wince when she quickly got her feet beneath her and stood. Pain shot up from her injured ankle through her leg, but she refused to favor it and show him any weakness. She would pay for it later, but every cell in her body yelled at her to get away as fast as she could.

She backed up several steps. "As I told you—*twice*—I want to be alone. You should get the hint when someone doesn't want your attention."

His smile vanished in an instant. One second, he was sitting. The next, he was before her. "And you shouldn't be so mean. Do you know what I am?"

"I don't give a damn who or what you are. I'm not interested." She knew there was no way she could get away from the Fae. He had magic, more than she could ever think to have. He'd be on top of her before she could get a running start. Why the hell had she come out here alone?

The Fae's silver eyes narrowed on her. "You look like someone who could use a good time. Come with me, and I'll give you pleasure, unlike any you've experienced."

"In your dreams." Sorcha inwardly kicked herself. The last thing she should be doing is purposefully irritating the Fae, but she couldn't seem to help herself.

In slow motion, she saw his hands reach for her. Before she could shove them aside or turn away, she caught a blur of movement out of the corner of her eye. The Fae fell over the waterfall in the next instant.

Sorcha then found herself staring at the back of a very tall, very broad-shouldered man with long, black and silver hair tied at his neck in a queue. It couldn't possibly be…. What were the odds that he'd be on Skye now?

Her mind froze, trying to come to terms with what she saw. Part of her wondered if she wanted this man to be the one from Ireland. Then she realized how stupid that sounded. She hadn't even gotten a good look at his face.

No, but you sure as hell felt his body. His very hard, very amazing body.

The man didn't turn to look at her. He walked to the edge of the waterfall and looked down before he jumped over the side. Unable to help herself, Sorcha rushed to edge and looked over to see the tall man beating the shite out of the Fae. The way the tall one moved, the way he had jumped over the side without hesitation, made her realize that he was Fae, as well. And with the silver in his hair, he was most likely Dark. The last thing she should do is get involved in any type of Fae dispute. Besides, the Druids would know about these two arriving. Perhaps she should get to Rhona and let her know exactly what had happened.

She glanced back to where her car was parked. It would take several minutes for her to get to her vehicle if she could run full out, and with her ankle, that wasn't possible. But she didn't want to wait around and find out who the man was. Did she?

The feel of the Irishman's thick muscles beneath her palms made her glance down again. She really wanted to see his face, to know if he was the man who had helped her in Ireland. But if he was, then it was likely no coincidence that he was on Skye. The last thing she should do is get mixed up with anything like this. She turned around to walk a couple of steps away.

But she couldn't leave. Her feet were rooted to the spot. She closed her eyes, trying to figure out what was wrong with her. She was doing everything opposite of what she had for the past ten years. It was like going to Ireland had swung her life around one hundred and eighty degrees. And she wasn't comfortable with it at all.

Her thoughts stilled as something hot and electric ran through her. It was the same sudden jolt that had gone through her in Ireland. Without looking behind her, she knew that the man was there. She could *feel* him.

For a full minute, neither said anything nor moved. Sorcha wasn't sure what she should do. She could probably walk away, and the man wouldn't say anything or even try to stop her. It would be the wise thing to do. The safe thing.

Wise? It might be more prudent to see who he is. If he is the same one who helped you in Ireland, there's a reason he's on Skye. It's always better to have information.

Maybe, but she didn't want to get involved. Getting answers meant that she would have to talk to people, and that totally messed up the hermit lifestyle she had come to know and love. All she had to do was lift her foot and move forward. Just lift the foot. It was simple. Liiiiiiift….

Instead, she turned around and found herself staring into the red eyes of a Dark Fae.

"I won't harm you," he said.

It was the same voice as the man in Ireland. She'd recognize it anywhere. Deep, velvety, and utterly erotic. She'd never heard another like it. Sorcha knew firsthand how stunningly beautiful all Fae were, regardless of if they were Light or Dark. This man was no exception. His face was cut from granite with hard edges that seemed to contrast with his full mouth, the bottom lip plumper than the top. His eyes were fringed with thick, black lashes. And his body…it looked just as good as it had felt beneath her hands the night he'd carried her.

But he was Fae. Dark Fae, at that.

His gaze slid away as he sighed. "I should've used glamour. I didn't mean to frighten you. That Light Fae won't be bothering you again."

CHAPTER SIX

"Why?"

Cathal blinked at her question. "Why, what?"

"Why did you help me? You're Dark."

It had never bothered him until that moment that he was a Dark Fae. He had accepted who he was long before he'd become a Reaper. Then again, she seemed to have been just as disgusted by the Light Fae. So maybe it wasn't only his coloring. "You told him twice to leave you alone."

"And you thought I needed saving. Again."

"If I hadn't stepped in, things could've gotten…bad…for you."

Her nostrils flared as she blew out a breath. "Thank you for helping me, but I didn't ask for it this time."

So, she did remember him. Cathal wasn't sure that was good or not. Any minute, she'd ask him how he had found her and what he wanted. He bowed his head, hoping to be gone before then. "I'll leave you so you can get back to whatever you were doing."

"Why are you here?"

He halted mid-stride. So much for him getting away before she dropped her questions. He looked at her, knowing that Aisling was near, veiled and listening. "Looking for you."

"Oh?" she said, brows raised. "Aren't I the lucky one? Whatever you want, I'm not interested."

"You might be if you listen to what I have to say."

She flattened her lips and shook her head. "I can guarantee I won't. The first time in ten years that I left my house was to go to Ireland. I did that as a favor, and I've regretted every minute of it."

"Really?" he asked. "For someone who hasn't left their house in that long, you seem to have enjoyed getting out enough to be here."

He didn't mention following her to the beach. It had gutted him to see her crying. He didn't know what had caused her tears, but the silent way she'd stood there as they ran down her face spoke of deep anguish. He recognized it since he had been there himself at one time.

Emerald green eyes narrowed for a heartbeat. "You're on Skye. The home of Druids. You might have access because of the Fairy Pools, but that doesn't mean your kind is welcome here."

At that, she turned on her heel and began to walk away.

Cathal smiled. She had spirit. There might be a thread of vulnerability in her, but courage and determination ran right alongside it. It would take a lot to break the Halfling. He respected that about her. Few people—mortals or Fae—had the strength to get through some of life's toughest hurdles. He might not know what the Halfling had been through, but based on her reactions, he suspected it was a whopper.

She had gotten about five meters from him when he said, "There's something you need to know."

Without stopping, she lifted a hand and said, "Keep it to yourself."

Just as Cathal was about to respond, he spotted a Light Fae that appeared just behind the Halfling. Cathal didn't give the Light a chance to speak. He teleported in front of the Fae and punched him in the face, knocking him out immediately. Cathal grabbed the Light before he could hit the ground. If the Halfling heard any of it, she didn't show it.

He glanced to the side to see Aisling standing next to him, still veiled. She jerked her chin toward the Halfling, letting Cathal know that she would follow her. Neither of them liked that two Fae had tried to approach her in such a short time. Normally, the Fae couldn't care less about a mortal who might have some Fae blood running through their veins. What was it about this Halfling that had brought attention to her?

Cathal gave one last look at the Halfling's retreating back. He wanted to continue talking with her, but that wasn't going to happen now. Aisling was more than capable of making sure the Halfling got home. In the meantime, Cathal was going to see if he could get some answers from the Light Fae he'd just stopped.

He attempted to wake the Fae. "Bloody hell. I guess I hit you harder than expected."

Cathal kept the Fae with him, tossing him over one shoulder like a sack as he walked around the Fairy Pools, veiled. To his surprise, four more Fae arrived. Most were Light, but there was a Dark also. As the sun rose higher, mortals began to appear, as well. The Fae didn't pay them any heed, even as some mortals blatantly let their interests be known.

When the Dark ignored a mortal, Cathal knew that something was up. The Fae were looking for something. And he had a sneaking suspicion that he knew what it was.

He took the unconscious Fae with him to the highest peak on Skye, where few people dared to venture. Then he dangled the Light by his foot over the side of the mountain and jiggled him a few times. It didn't take long for the Fae to wake.

"About time," Cathal said. "I want answers."

"Who the fek are you?" the Fae asked as he tilted his head while crunching his torso to try and see Cathal.

Cathal raised a brow. "Since I'm not the one being held upside down over a mountain, I'll be the one asking the questions."

"I'm not answering anything. Especially not to a Dark."

Cathal twisted his lips as he nodded. "Fair enough. But if you aren't going to talk, then that means there's no use for you." As he finished speaking, he held out his hand and called his sword to him.

The Fae lived exceptionally long years. But they could be killed. Especially by a blade forged in the Fires of Erwar.

The Light held up his hands. "Whoa. Hold on. Let's not be hasty."

"It took too long for you to wake, and you're making this difficult. My patience is wearing thin. You've got one chance to tell me what I want to know, or I'll end your life."

Since Death hadn't sent Cathal to reap this Fae's soul, he couldn't actually kill him. But Cathal kept that tidbit of information to himself.

"Fine. Ask your questions," the Light said hastily, his voice laced with exasperation.

Cathal smiled. "What do you want with the Halfling?"

The Light let out a loud sigh and relaxed his midsection. "Of course, you'd ask that."

"I'm waiting," Cathal stated.

"Fine! You want to know who she is?" the Fae asked as he crunched his torso again. "She's the reason the Fae will begin flocking to this isle over the next few days."

Cathal frowned, not liking what he was hearing. "Why?"

"You're a Fae!" The Light shook his head in annoyance. "You should know. Look, mate, the bloodline of that family is like a blessing from the gods. If a male can impregnate one of them, that Fae and his family are guaranteed to always be able to return to this realm, even if we're forced to leave."

"You're full of shite."

"I'm not," he said and shook his head of black hair. "Why do you think she's a Halfling? The family learned of this long ago, and they do a ritual every year to keep them safe from us. But every female of that family must be involved in the ritual. That Halfling hasn't done a ritual in ten years. This is the first year she left the safety of her home. And I'm going to be the one to plant my seed in her."

Red filled Cathal's vision. "You're going to leave Skye. And you're going to let every Fae know that the Halfling isn't to be touched."

"Because you want her for yourself," the Light said, his gaze narrowed in anger.

Cathal brought the blade of his sword against the Fae's throat. "The only thing you need to be concerned with is getting away from me with your life. If I see you again on this isle or anywhere near that Halfling, I'll gut you from your nose to your balls. Do you understand me?"

The Fae nodded quickly. "I understand perfectly."

"You better. You don't want me hunting you down." Cathal tossed him to the side.

The Fae rolled before he jumped to his feet. He didn't look back at Cathal as he teleported away. Cathal immediately veiled himself and jumped to the Halfling's house, where he found Aisling sitting on the porch, still veiled. The moment she saw him, she rose and walked to him.

"This isle is crawling with Fae," she said when she reached him.

Cathal nodded, his lips flattening. "I found out why." He then told her what he'd discovered.

Her red eyes grew large. "What the hell? I've never heard of this Halfling's family or that crock of shite."

"Me either," Cathal said with a shrug. "But someone must know of it. Otherwise, the Fae wouldn't be coming here."

Aisling glanced over her shoulder at the cottage. "I looked all over the outside of the house. I can't find any symbols that would keep a Fae out."

"Nothing kept us out, but the same rules don't apply to Reapers."

"If there are no wards to keep the Fae out, then they can get to her in her cottage."

Cathal twisted his lips. "I'm not so sure of that. The Light I spoke with made a point of saying that this was the first time the Halfling had left her property in ten years."

Aisling's face registered shock. "I don't buy that at all. She's had to leave at least once a month for supplies."

"I don't know. Even the Halfling made mention of not leaving for a while. Maybe there is something to that." He glanced around. "Perhaps the property itself is protected. This is the home of the Skye Druids, after all."

"Something isn't adding up, that's for sure," Aisling said as she crossed her arms over her chest.

Cathal couldn't argue with that. "Looks like we have more information to gather."

"I'll do that. You stay and talk to the Halfling."

He frowned. "I'm not sure that's wise."

"She's not going to want to talk to another Fae. You've got some kind of rapport with her. Use it. I don't think we have time for me or anyone else to get close to her."

Cathal had to admit that Aisling was right. He felt as if their time was running out, and he wasn't even sure why or for what. "Watch your back out there."

She laughed and clicked her long red nails. "I dare anyone to fek with me. Have fun with your Halfling." Then, she was gone.

Cathal found himself smiling even after Aisling had left. She wasn't particularly easy to get to know. Then again, none of the Reapers were. Aisling kept to herself, but over the last few months, he had seen her do little things that proved that she was coming to bond with the Reapers. It made it easy on Death's realm, where no one but the Reapers and their mates lived.

When Kyran's mate, River, had birthed their child, everyone had wanted to see the first baby born to a Reaper. None of the men had stepped up to hold the child. But Aisling had. There had been a look on her face that had caught everyone's attention. Aisling hadn't seemed to care. She cooed to the infant for a little while before handing her back to River.

As far as Cathal knew, Aisling hadn't been back to see the baby. But there was a vase full of different colored flowers outside of the infant's window every week. Or at least that's what Kyran told them.

Cathal's attention returned to the Halfling and the cottage. Then he moved his gaze around, looking to see if any Fae were near. So far, nothing. But that didn't mean they wouldn't come. Is that what had happened to the Halfling's mother? Had she been cornered and taken advantage of by a Fae?

The thought made him sick.

Mortals were drawn to Fae like moths to a flame. There was no getting around it. It wasn't as if the Fae had made themselves that way. It's just how it was. Some Fae didn't like how much attention they got from mortals, so they used glamour to hide their beauty and magic to tone down their appeal.

However, most Fae gloried in the devotion. Because humans fawned over them like gods. Cathal had seen it many times. Even when the mortals were purposefully drawn to a place like the Dark Palace and kept prisoner to be used sexually, they didn't seem to care. Their only thought was to feel the pleasure that being in the arms of a Fae guaranteed.

Even as the soul of the human was being taken from them with every sexual act. They died with a smile on their faces.

That's why the Dark Fae—and some Light—didn't consider draining a mortal murder. They argued that if someone died with a smile, it couldn't be bad. It was a load of shite. The Dark took great pleasure in taking the humans' souls. The Light were allowed to sleep with a mortal once, thinking that didn't do as much damage. The opposite was true. Once a human had sex with a Fae, no other mortal could live up to them—or satisfy the human. The mortal was irrevocably ruined.

Cathal grimaced. The Halfling clearly didn't like Fae. He had a sneaking suspicion that it had to do with her lineage. The tears she'd cried earlier most likely had to do with her mother. But the Halfling was in her late twenties at a minimum. So, she hadn't lost her mother at an early age. Or had she? There were so many unanswered questions. Cathal wished he knew the answers for some of them. Then maybe he'd be able to talk to her.

He sighed and walked around the cottage, taking in the flowering bushes, hanging baskets with colored petals draped over the sides, and even windowsill planter boxes with flowers. The house sat atop a hill, looking out in all directions over pastures, mountains, and in the distance, water. A small herb plot rested near the house. Next to it was a vegetable patch. Beyond that, a flower garden.

The sheer abundance of flowers and plants and how well they grew reminded him of the first time he'd gone to Death's realm. Erith had a thing for flowers, and the plants seemed to bloom as she neared, as if they were eager for her attention.

Cathal found himself walking among the flora. There were posies, lavender, hollyhocks, and delphinium. He saw an outside table area that was covered with wisteria, growing all over it to keep it shaded. Then he spotted the rose garden. Cathal couldn't help but take a closer look. There were blooms of every size and color. This section was twice the size of the other gardens, and the fragrance hung heavy in the air.

He was just turning away when he happened to see a weathered stick helping to support one of the rose bushes. It was only by chance that he caught what looked like writing on the one-inch thick wood. He leaned closer, but it was so worn that he couldn't make it out clearly. That's when he ran his finger over it and traced the small outline of a ward used to keep Fae out.

It was the first sign of any ward he'd seen. Aisling had searched the property, but she probably hadn't thought to look in the gardens. He wouldn't have either. It had been sheer luck that he'd even spotted it.

He straightened and looked over the plants to the cottage. The marking was old. Very old. It was wearing thin as well, which meant that the ward wasn't strong. That could allow a powerful Fae to come onto the land. How much would it take to enter the house? Cathal walked around the dwelling again. This time, he looked at inconspicuous places to search for the wards. Unfortunately, he didn't find any.

Cathal ran a hand down his face and blew out a breath. Out of the corner of his eye, he saw movement. When he looked, he found a Fae on the neighboring property, looking at the Halfling's cottage. Cathal was about to go to the Fae when he realized that he couldn't take the time to chase each and every Fae away. While he was occupied with one, others could rush the house.

That left him with only one option.

He walked to the front of the house and onto the porch. Then he dropped his veil and knocked on the door.

CHAPTER SEVEN

The last thing Sorcha expected was a knock on her door. She jerked her head up from making tea and stared at the front of the house as if willing herself to see through it and to who wanted to talk to her. She didn't move. Her ankle was swollen again from her hike at the pools. She just wanted to lay on the couch and pretend that the morning hadn't happened.

The knock came again.

She turned her head. If she ignored whoever it was, maybe they would go away. She knew it wasn't Rhona, because her cousin would've called to let her know that she was here. Whoever had come was a stranger, which meant, Sorcha didn't want to answer the door and pretend to be nice. And the very last thing she wanted was to invite anyone in.

Minutes went by with nothing. Sorcha let out a sigh. Finally, something had gone right.

Then came the knock once more.

She dropped her chin to her chest. Was this Fate laughing at her? Telling her that it didn't matter what she wanted, that she had to go to the door?

Fuck Fate. I've had enough. I just want to be left alone.

"I'm going to keep knocking until you open the door."

Her stomach fell to her feet. She knew that voice. It was seared into her brain from the other night, and then just a little while ago at the pools. But what was the Irishman doing at her house? And how the hell had he found her?

She forgot about wanting to be alone and hobbled her way to the door. Without opening it, she said, "I told you I didn't want to hear what you had to say."

"That no longer matters. The simple fact is, the Fae are interested in you. And they'll stop at nothing to get you."

Sorcha frowned, not liking the feeling his words gave her. "This is Skye. Nothing can happen to me here."

A long, drawn-out sigh reached her. "I wish I could say you're right, but that isn't the case. You don't want to see me, and I respect that. But at least let me say my piece. Then, I'll go."

Could it be that easy? She knew it wasn't. Nothing ever was. People said whatever they needed to get what they wanted. She didn't trust anyone. Well, that wasn't exactly true. She trusted Rhona. Partly because she was family, and in part because Sorcha had known Rhona her entire life.

"My name is Cathal," he said. "I give you my word that I'm not here to harm you. I could've done that in Ireland or a little while ago at the Fairy Pools. I did neither."

Sorcha put her forehead against the door, her ankle throbbing. "Well, Cathal, that's all very nice, but I don't trust anything you're saying."

"Good," he replied.

That made her pause. "What's that supposed to mean?"

"Exactly what I said. You shouldn't trust anyone. I don't care if you crack a window and we talk through it, but I need to speak with you."

"Then talk here."

"I'd rather see your face."

Sorcha frowned and looked longingly at the chair near the window. She could sit down and prop up her ankle to help with the pain. That's what she had been making the herbal tea for. She couldn't listen to him and deal with the agony, not as the throbbing intensified. "Can we do this later? Tomorrow, perhaps?"

"It needs to be now."

If it would get him to go away, then she'd listen to his nonsense. Sorcha used the furniture she passed as a crutch to get to the chair. She opened the window a few inches after she sat. "Cathal," she called.

In two strides, he was there, looking down at her with his red eyes. Sorcha realized belatedly that she should be shocked that a Dark Fae was speaking with her. She'd seen one from afar before, but this was her first time speaking with one so close. She knew how dangerous they could be, which made her question her sanity for being so gruff with him. What kind of deranged person intentionally angered a Dark Fae?

Apparently, she did.

She inwardly rolled her eyes at herself. It would probably do her a world of good to talk to a therapist. Then again, would it really help to rehash things that only made her want to curl into a ball and pretend that the world around her didn't exist? Not really.

Cathal pulled one of the rocking chairs from the porch around and sank onto it. Sorcha waited for the wood to groan in protest at his considerable height, but to her surprise, there was nothing. She watched a lock of hair that escaped his queue dance around his face before tangling in his thick eyelashes. Her fringe never looked like that, even with mascara. Thanks to her auburn locks, her lashes were all but nonexistent.

"Thank you," he said.

She shrugged and shifted to lift her leg. "What is it you want?"

His gaze looked through the glass to her ankle. "Is that still bothering you?"

"Naw. I just like to pretend I have an injury."

Jesus Christ! What the bloody hell is wrong with you, Sorcha? You're never this vile to anyone. I wouldn't blame him at all for punching through the glass and thumping your head.

She grimaced as she looked away. "I'm sorry. I don't know what's wrong with me."

"You've had a rough morning," he said calmly.

Sorcha blinked and looked into his eyes. He didn't appear miffed with her at all. She had an awful habit of becoming sarcastic and snotty when she was in a foul mood. Still, that didn't excuse her behavior. "It doesn't explain my attitude. You didn't deserve that. I have had a rough morning, and my ankle is killing me, but I know better than to take it out on others. You have, in fact, saved me twice. And I repaid you with attitude. I'm beyond remorseful."

"How about you repay me with two things? Listen to what I have to say, and tell me your name."

That was an easy request. She found her lips softening into a smile. So many times, she'd said that she hated the Irish accent, but there was something about Cathal's that sounded nice to her ears. Whether it was the deep timbre or his smooth intonation, she found herself easing back in the chair. "Deal. My name is Sorcha."

"Hello, Sorcha," he said with a grin that made her heart skip a beat.

She'd always hated her name. Yet, the moment it rolled off his tongue, her blood heated, and she found it difficult to breathe. She blinked, unable to look away from his gorgeous face. It had been easier to attempt to ignore him when it had been raining, when she walked away from him, and when she'd been talking to him through a door. Now, face-to-face, with nothing but glass between them, she felt as if she were drowning in his crimson eyes.

"You can fix your ankle," he said.

She licked her lips and shrugged. "I don't do magic anymore."

He frowned slightly, and his brows drew together. "I'm sorry to hear that. If you'd like, I can fix it. There's no need for you to be in pain."

"Why would you offer that to someone you barely know?"

"Because it was Fate that our paths crossed. It was Fate that brought me to this isle to find you. Whether our destinies go different ways after today or not, we were meant to meet. You have the ability to heal yourself, and for whatever reason, you choose not to. I respect that. Let me do it."

Sorcha didn't know what to do. She couldn't look away from his gaze. She was trapped, ensnared. Caught. And she wasn't too upset about any of it. Maybe she'd spent so much time alone that she had lost the ability to tell if someone was decent or not. Surely, having a conversation with a Dark Fae was the most outrageous, ludicrous thing she'd ever done. And now, he'd offered to heal her. A Dark.

She knew she should decline, and yet she found herself nodding. Cathal put the tips of his fingers under the edge of the open window and gave her a nod. Sorcha gingerly lifted her injured ankle to the windowsill until his fingers touched her skin. The moment they made contact, chills raced over her. Right on the heels of that, heat seared her veins. All the while, their gazes remained locked.

Cathal's lips didn't move. There was no vocal spell that came from him. Seconds turned to minutes. Finally, he pulled his hand away. "There you go."

To say she was disappointed that he no longer touched her was an understatement. Obviously, she'd been on her own for too long if she were getting excited—and turned on—by the brush of a man's hands on her skin.

He did more than brush your skin. He's held you. Tightly. You know just how good that hard body feels against yours. How strong. How utterly f—

"Does it feel better?"

She startled at his voice. Then slowly moved her ankle. There was no pain. She set her foot on the floor and stood. Walked around. When she came back to the chair, she flashed him a wide smile. "Thank you. I feared I had done more damage to it this morning by going to the pools."

"I'm glad I could help."

"Forgive me, but I don't think I've ever known a Dark to willingly help a mortal like this."

He lifted his broad shoulders in a shrug. "I'm not like other Dark."

She had already guessed that. "All right. You wanted to talk. I suppose you better get on with it."

His red gaze slid away briefly. "What I have to say won't be easy for you to hear."

"That's usually the case, isn't it?" She sat back, the happiness she'd felt swiftly leaving. She liked him, and she knew that whatever he was about to tell her would likely make that change. He was the first person she'd spoken to in years that wasn't family or someone on the isle. Even when she went to Ireland, she hadn't spoken more than a handful of words to the B&B owner. She didn't consider that a conversation.

This, what she was doing with Cathal, was definitely a conversation. And it felt good. Not only was he drop-dead gorgeous, but he had also helped her—three times now. He appeared to be a decent fellow. If one could call a Dark Fae *decent*.

"You say you're a Druid," Cathal began.

Sorcha nodded. "Because I am."

"Why do you say that?"

She laughed as she rolled her eyes. "Because my mother was. My sister was. And I have magic."

"What of your father?"

Immediately, Sorcha was on guard. "What about him?"

"Was he a Druid?"

"No. He was just someone passing through town that got my mother pregnant. It was a one-night stand, if you must know."

"What about your sister?"

Sorcha's brows snapped together. "My sister was older. Her father, my mother's husband, died."

Cathal nodded as his gaze lowered to the ground. "I'm sorry to hear that."

"Why does any of that matter?"

He drew in a deep breath and looked up at her. "Because you're a Halfling. You have Fae blood running through your veins."

CHAPTER EIGHT

The stillness that came over Sorcha was something even a blind man would notice. Cathal's fingers still tingled from touching her ankle. He wanted nothing more than to reach through the few inches of the open window and touch her again. While they talked, she had relaxed.

Now, the wall that had been around her before had gone back up in record time—higher and thicker than ever before. Cathal regretted how he'd told her, but there hadn't been another way. He'd thought it easier to just give it to her straight. Ripping off the Band-Aid, as he'd heard so many mortals say.

He licked his lips. "I'm sure this comes as a shock to you."

"You're lying," she stated.

"I'm not. A Fae knows another Fae."

Sorcha shook her head of auburn curls. "I'm a Druid."

"Actually, you're a Halfling, who happens to also be a Druid. The fact that you come from such powerful Druids is something that hasn't happened before."

"You think?" she retorted angrily. Then, with her face and voice full of sarcasm, she said, "And I wonder why that is?"

Cathal shifted uncomfortably. He really wished Aisling was with him. She'd know what to say right now. He wasn't good at talking. He always messed it up by saying the wrong thing. "Is it so bad having Fae blood?"

"More than you could possibly imagine."

Her words were laced with such hatred that it took him aback. If she felt that strongly, why had she allowed him to have a conversation?

Sorcha pushed angrily to her feet. Without looking at him, she said, "You've said what you wanted. You need to leave."

"I'm not finished. There's more."

"I don't bloody care. Leave!"

He noticed her hands fisted at her sides. She shook with emotion. Her gaze was directed away from him, but he saw that her jaw was clenched, and she was doing everything she could to keep herself from falling apart.

Cathal slowly got to his feet. "When you're ready to hear the rest, just say my name. I'll come immediately. And…I'm sorry. I never meant to upset you."

He waited a few seconds, but Sorcha wouldn't look at him. Cathal drew in a deep breath and walked away. He didn't get two steps before the window slammed shut behind him. The moment he got to the edge of the porch, he veiled himself and looked back at her. She no longer stood at the window. Cathal hated that he'd caused her stress, but there was no way around it. Besides, there had been a chance that she would've taken the news as something to celebrate.

There was no way to look at this that would give him any kind of reprieve. He was the one who had wanted to seek Sorcha out. He had wanted to speak with her. And what had it gotten him? Not a bloody thing.

During the next hour, Cathal guarded the property. More and more Fae showed up. Some stayed, others hid, and a few seemed content just to make sure Sorcha was there. But not one of them realized there were Reapers on the isle—or guarding Sorcha.

When Aisling returned, Cathal had never been happier to see her. "About time."

She gave him an odd look. "I thought you wanted some alone time with the Halfling."

"Sorcha."

Aisling smiled. "Ah. You found out her name. Does that mean you spoke with her?"

"Aye."

"I take that to mean it didn't go well."

He ran a hand down his face. "Not at all. It started off all right. She wouldn't use her magic to heal her ankle, but she allowed me to do it."

"Wow. That did start out well. How did you fek it up?"

Cathal couldn't take offense at her words because they were the truth. "I asked about her family. She said she was a Druid, that her mother and sister were, as well. She said her sister's father died, and her mother met someone else and became pregnant with her."

Aisling's nose wrinkled in a grimace. "Is that when you told her she's a Halfling?"

"I thought it was the perfect opportunity."

"Well, to be fair, I probably would've done the same. Especially if the conversation had been going well up to that point."

Cathal looked at the cottage. No matter how many times he walked around the house, he hadn't seen more than a glimpse of her within. "She hates Fae."

"Damn. Wait," Aisling said, a frown creasing her brow. "If she hates us, why did she speak with you?"

He shrugged. "I wondered that myself. She wouldn't come

outside or let me in, but she opened a window a bit so we could talk. Then she let me heal her. Please tell me you found out something."

"I did, but before I get to that, what the hell?" she asked as she turned her head one way and then the other, taking in the Fae who had shown up but weren't stepping onto Sorcha's property.

"I spotted the first one not long after you left. I also found a worn ward against the Fae in the rose garden. It's on a piece of weathered wood."

"Which means it's losing its effectiveness," Aisling said.

Cathal nodded as he eyed the Fae who had been there the longest. "I checked around the entire property again, but that's the only ward I found."

"There could be more inside the house."

"Could be."

"Want me to look?"

He hesitated to answer. It would be easy for both of them to get inside the cottage as they'd done earlier, but he didn't want to invade Sorcha's privacy—even if it was to protect her.

Aisling held up a hand. "I understand. We might not have a choice later, though."

"I don't know what it is about Sorcha."

The Dark female shrugged and looked away. "You don't have to try and explain anything to me. I'm the last person who will judge you."

Cathal's gaze slid to her. He studied her profile for a moment before he said, "Thank you."

"It's nothing," she said offhandedly.

But he knew otherwise.

Aisling cleared her throat and faced him. "As tightknit as the residents on Skye are, they are quite the gossips."

"They talked to you about Sorcha?"

"No," Aisling said with a roll of her red eyes. "I ventured into a pub veiled. It was full of locals, and the main topic of conversation was none other than Sorcha. Well, her and the fact that, apparently, they have spells up that alert them when any Fae arrive."

Cathal crossed his arms over his chest, not liking that people were talking about Sorcha.

Aisling gave him a flat look. "Don't get your panties in a wad. If they hadn't been talking about her, I wouldn't have found out anything. Besides, they weren't badmouthing her."

That made him feel a little better. Not much, but some. "What did they say?"

"Turns out, she didn't lie. Until a few days ago, when she agreed to go to Ireland to spy, Sorcha hadn't left her property in ten years. Nor does she do magic."

"But why?" Cathal asked, confused.

Aisling's lips flattened for a heartbeat. "I didn't learn the story behind it, but apparently, it has something to do with the day her mother and sister died."

"That would explain why she got restless when she spoke about her family."

"I gather it's a sore subject." Aisling shrugged. "I tried to uncover the story, but it isn't something anyone talks about."

Cathal dropped his arms to his sides as he blew out a breath. "That explains a lot, actually. I wish I would've known all of that before I talked to her."

"It's probably better that you didn't. Whatever happened to her family…it left a raw wound that doesn't appear to have healed. Take my advice and don't bring it up again. If Sorcha wants to talk about it, then she'll bring it up."

Cathal nodded as he looked at the cottage, wondering what Sorcha was doing. "You're probably right."

"I know I'm right. Do you want to talk about your past?"

His head snapped to her as his brows drew together. "Fek no."

"Then she won't either. No one likes to talk about a past as dark and horrid as ours. I've got a sneaking suspicion hers is just as bad."

"Fek me," Cathal said as he turned away and walked a few paces before he stopped.

Aisling walked to him. "You told her what needed to be said."

"I didn't finish. As soon as I informed her she was a Halfling, she ordered me to leave. I told her I'd be around when she was ready to hear the rest."

"The rest? Ah. You mean about the ritual. She does need to know about that."

He twisted his lips as he met Aisling's gaze. "You have any ideas?"

"Other than beating the hell out of the Fae who think they can come onto this property? None. I don't think there's anything more we can do at this time. At least not until Sorcha wants to hear more."

"If she ever does."

Aisling looked over her shoulder at the cottage. "Maybe she'll surprise us. At least the Druids here are aware of the Fae's arrival. Though they can't do anything about it. Not sure it'll even help Sorcha."

What worried him more was how long he and Aisling would be able to stay on Skye before Death called them back.

"Look, big guy," Aisling said as she slapped him on the arm. "It's going to be all right. It always is."

He couldn't say that it always turned out okay. In fact, he was pretty sure it didn't. But he didn't argue with Aisling. She was trying to help him, so he left it at that.

She cracked her knuckles. "So, which side of the property do you want?"

"You pick first," he answered with a grin.

If there was one thing Reapers knew how to do, it was fight. It was one of the main reasons Erith had chosen each of them.

Aisling looked at the Fae who had arrived first. He was a big Light Fae that had yet to take his eyes off the cottage. "I don't like the looks of him."

"Neither do I."

"Well, perhaps it's time someone urged him to leave."

Cathal shook his head as he caught her gaze. "Let's not touch any of them unless they come on the property."

She rolled her eyes. "You take all the fun out of everything."

But there was a smile on her face as she started toward the Light Fae. Once she had taken her position, Cathal took his. There was no way any Fae would get near Sorcha now—or ever.

CHAPTER NINE

He was wrong. He had to be.

Sorcha repeated that over and over in her head after Cathal had walked away. She was glad he'd left, as well as irritated that he had gone so easily. He should've forced her to listen to whatever else he had to say.

"Right. Because that would've gone over so well," she said to herself, sighing loudly in exasperation.

The problem was that she had been having a good time with him. A very good time, in fact. She hadn't been prepared for his words—or how they affected her. Half-Fae. That couldn't be possible. Could it?

No matter how many times she asked herself that, there was no answer. In fact, the only one who could answer that was her mum. And since she was dead, how else could Sorcha learn the truth? Then, it hit her.

She hurried to her mother's room. Sorcha had left things decorated as they were. She might have changed up the rest of the house, but her mother's and sister's bedrooms, as well as everything inside, had been left as they were. Sorcha was glad that she'd made that decision years ago because there just might be something in here that could help.

For the next few hours, she opened every drawer, looked through every box, but didn't find anything to give her any clue as to who her father had been. Sorcha remembered being young and asking about her dad. Her mother hadn't turned her away or tried to talk of other things. She'd been very open about it and said that she'd met him one night, and their passion had been undeniable. They'd had a brief affair before he left. It was only once he was gone that she learned she was pregnant—and had no way to get in touch with him.

Sorcha sat on the bed, letting that conversation run through her head. The one thing she'd never asked her mum was the name of her father. Her mother had talked about her dead husband and Sorcha's father in generalities often. Maybe that's why it had never dawned on her to ask her mother what his name was. In this day and age of electronics, it wouldn't have been difficult to find him.

Unless her mum couldn't locate him because he was Fae.

Sorcha covered her face with her hands. There was no reason for Cathal to lie to her. Or was there? She dropped her hands and lifted her head. The Fae had proven time and again that they couldn't be trusted.

And humans haven't?

"Shut up," she told her subconscious.

The last thing she needed was to argue with herself. Unfortunately, now that the words had been said, she couldn't stop thinking about them. She believed Cathal. Not because he was so good-looking, it was sinful. But because there had been sincerity in his face, eyes, and voice. Of course, there was a chance that he could be a great liar, but she didn't think so.

Sorcha rose and walked to the doorway. She was about to click off the light when she glanced at the bed. That's when she remembered seeing her mother putting something in between the mattress and box spring when she was a little girl. Sorcha hurried to the bed, shoved aside the comforter, and lifted the mattress. That's when she spotted six different journals.

She grabbed them all and took them with her into the living room. A glance through the windows showed that it had grown dark. She quickly pulled the curtains and sat cross-legged on the sofa as she found the earliest journal and opened it.

It started the day her mum buried her husband. Sorcha could barely read the words penned with such grief and despair that it brought tears to her eyes. Her mother had loved her husband dearly. His death had been sudden and tragic. The only thing that'd seemed to pull her mother through was Sorcha's sister, Molly. That journal was full of days of heartache and depression with a few good days sprinkled throughout.

The second journal began a year to the day after her mother's husband's death. Sorcha quickly realized that her mum had gone through a lot that year, forcing herself to look ahead instead of into the past. She focused on Molly and being the best mom she could. Men asked her out, but her mum always refused.

The third journal started out much the same, but something changed midway through. Her mum went from trying to find something to be happy about, to *being* happy. She never mentioned a man by name, but it was obvious that there was someone. Their meeting was nine months to the day before Sorcha's birth. Unfortunately, her mother didn't speak much about the man.

July 18th

· · ·

I saw him again. What is it about him that draws me? I can't seem to stay away. I honestly believed I would never love again after my husband, but now I see there's a chance. A real *chance.*

I'd love to introduce him to my sister and Molly, but I can't bear to share him with anyone right now. This is too new. And even though I know he's leaving soon, I hope that I can convince him to stay forever. We're good together. Even he's said that. He doesn't want to leave. I don't want him to go.

What's happening between us is very sudden. And yet, I know it's real. How could something this strong, this amazing be anything but real? I should fear how fast all of this is moving, but I don't. I know in my heart it's right. We're meant to be together.

While I don't want to leave Skye, I'd go anywhere to be with him. He's my future. The person I'll spend my days with once Molly is out on her own. For the first time, I see a real future for myself. Someone who will stand beside me and share my life. A father for Molly, and maybe, just maybe, more children.

I can't stop smiling. I've only known him for two weeks, but they have been the best two weeks of my life. When a person finds their soulmate, they know. And I knew the moment I looked at him. It was electric.

I'm about to go meet him in our usual spot. We keep our love hidden from everyone, because many wouldn't understand. I don't care what others think. I just know what I feel.

Sorcha bit her lip as she reread the last paragraph. Could her mother have been trying to say that her love was Fae? There was an argument for that. It could also mean that he wasn't a Druid. What was obvious was that the man wasn't from Skye, and that was all Sorcha could decipher for certain.

She read a few more pages where her mother continued to speak about how happy she was. The entries took place over the course of a month. Then she came to the next page.

August 12th

I knew this day was coming, and I'd thought I prepared. But nothing could have prepared me for what I felt when he left. I can't stop crying. My sister keeps asking me what's wrong. I promised him I wouldn't tell anyone about us, but it's so difficult. I'm bereft without him. He's taken my heart with him.

At least he promised to return as soon as he can. When he does, he said we'll be together forever. Since he has others he needs to answer to just as I do, I'm trying to be patient. What's a few months when we'll have years together?

I know that, and yet, I can't stop feeling as if I'll never see him again.

Sorcha hesitated before she read the next few passages.

September 2nd

I'm pregnant! I can't wait to tell him. He's going to be so thrilled. Our family will have grown by one when he returns. The only way I could be happier is if he was here to share the news with.

November 29th

He was supposed to be back by now. I'm getting worried. I've had to lie to my family and tell them I had a one-night stand with a tourist. I kept putting off telling them anything, hoping he'd return. Then I started showing, and I had to tell them something. Molly is excited. She keeps telling me she's going to have a sister.

January 5th

That feeling I had that I'd never see him again grows each day that he doesn't return. I keep a little hope that I'm wrong, but I know I'm not. I already lost one man I loved. Now, it seems as if I've lost a second. Maybe I'm cursed.

My sister would probably say I was suckered, but she'd be wrong. If she had experienced everything I did with him, then she'd understand. She would see that he didn't lie or use me. He loved me as much as I loved him. We vowed to spend the rest of our lives together. Magic bound us. He never would've done that if he didn't mean it.

April 20th

My beautiful Sorcha was born today. She, like Molly, will grow up without a father, but that's all right. I will love my girls enough to make up for it. And I'll make sure both of them know enough about their fathers so they don't think I'm hiding things.

I wish I could tell Sorcha everything. Perhaps one day I will. Until then, the secrets will stay with me, buried alongside my broken heart. She's a Skye Druid. The Druids born on Skye are very powerful. No one will think twice about how much magic she has. Skye is the safest place for her. Until she's ready to know the truth.

Sorcha felt as if she'd been punched in the gut. She read the last passage over and over again. It didn't outright say that she had Fae blood, but there was enough there to allude to it. She dashed away the tears that fell onto her cheeks and hurriedly read the rest of the journal entries. No more did her mum mention her magic, secrets, or the man who hadn't come back for her.

By the time Sorcha closed the last journal, she had more questions than when she'd first started reading. What was it that her mother had wanted her to know? And why did it matter if a Skye Druid and a Fae found love? Nothing said that a Druid couldn't be with a Fae. For most of Sorcha's life, the Fae were revered on Skye. It had only been recently with the mess with the Others and Usaeil that things had gone south.

Now, it was well known that being with a Fae could ruin a person from having a relationship with a mortal. Sorcha had used to scoff at that. In fact, she and her friends had once said they would rather have a Fae since their choices for mortals were…lacking.

Sorcha gathered the journals and rose to carry them back to her mother's room. She didn't put them between the mattress. Instead, she put them on the shelf in the closet. On her way back to the living room, she passed the chair she'd sat in to speak to Cathal and was reminded how he'd healed her ankle.

He had promised to tell her the rest of what he'd come to say. She wasn't sure what that could be, but she couldn't help but be curious about it. There was so much about her past that had been kept a secret from her. Her life had been so normal, that it had never dawned on her that she was different from her sister. From an early age, she remembered her mother practicing magic with both her and Molly.

Sorcha could go back to burying her head in the sand as she had for ten years. Or she could call for Cathal and find out the rest. Once she heard everything from him, she would then dig into her past and see what else she could discover. Maybe Rhona knew something. Someone had to know *something*. She wasn't just going to take Cathal's word for it. He was a Dark, after all.

Then, it hit her. Her father might have been Dark. Is that why Cathal had sought her out?

"Bloody hell. Is he my father?"

She hoped to hell not because it would be really awkward to be attracted to her sire. Sorcha put that out of her mind before she made herself sick. Then she walked around the coffee table, weighing her options before she finally stopped.

After a deep breath, she said, "Cathal."

In the next instant, there was a knock on the door. "It's me," he called.

She licked her lips and walked to the door before she unbolted it and opened it. The minute her gaze landed on him, the tension inside her began to ease.

"I'm glad you called for me."

"Come in," she beckoned as she stepped aside.

He walked past her into the house before he turned and waited as she closed the door and faced him. "Are you all right?"

"No," she said with a half-laugh. "I dug through my mother's journals to see if I could find anything. She mentioned a man that she'd met. They hid their affair. She doesn't mention that he's a Fae, nor does she note his name."

Cathal's red eyes held a hint of sorrow. "That must have been difficult to read."

"He promised to come back for her, but he never did. My mum talked about him when I was younger, but it never dawned on me to ask his name. Maybe because Molly, my sister, never asked her dad's name. Of course, we knew it, but…" She trailed off and shrugged. "Looking back, I don't know why I didn't ask. Is there any way you can find out if he was Fae?"

"I—" he began hesitantly.

Sorcha held up a hand and shook her head. "I'm sorry. I had no right to ask that. Forget I said anything."

CHAPTER TEN

There was no way Cathal could forget a single syllable Sorcha said. Ever. She was being torn in two, and he hated that he was adding to it.

"It's not that I don't want to help. It's that I'm not sure I'll find out anything," he told her. "But I'll ask around."

She smiled. "That's kind of you, especially after how I've treated you."

"It's never easy to learn your world has been turned upside down."

"No, it isn't. Where are my manners? Please, sit."

They walked to the living area. Cathal waited until she chose the chair before he lowered himself into a corner of the sofa. She shifted a few times, trying to get comfortable through her nervousness. It made him want to smile.

"I guess it would be better if you just finished telling me what you tried earlier," Sorcha said.

Cathal put an ankle over his knee and rested his elbow on the arm of the sofa. "The Fae that spoke with you at the Fairy Pools? There are more gathering around the isle, waiting for you."

"Me?" she asked with a frown. "Why? Because I'm half-Fae?"

"I don't think the fact you're a Halfling plays into it at all. This is about your family's bloodline. From what I gathered from a Fae I spoke with today, if one of them can plant his seed within you, then they'll be able to return if the Fae are ever booted from this realm. Because of their child with your bloodline."

Sorcha's frown increased as she blinked, trying to take it all in. "That doesn't make sense at all. Why just me? Why not my cousin, Rhona?"

"Because you've not done the ritual. Apparently, you must take part every year."

"Bloody hell," she murmured as her face smoothed out in shock. "Everyone always talked about that damn ritual, but there are so many. All of them are touted as important, but I never learned the reasons."

Cathal nodded. "And you didn't want to leave the house."

"That was part of it, yes," she admitted.

He waited, hoping she'd say more, but she didn't. "You chose not to do the ritual. I'm guessing that had something to do with you not wanting to do magic anymore."

Her gaze darted away as she took a deep breath, green eyes flashing. Then she looked at him once more. "As far back as I can remember, my mother taught me magic. My sister, Molly, and I spent hours doing it, perfecting our skills and learning spells."

"Magic came easily to you," he guessed.

"Very. Mum cautioned both of us constantly on how to use magic and when to use it. Molly didn't struggle with it, but she didn't always catch on as easily as I did."

Cathal nodded slowly. "You never thought you were more than a Druid?"

"Never. Mum never singled me out for doing magic better than Molly. Nor did Mum ever pull me aside and tell me she was worried about the magic I used. Perhaps it would've been better if she had."

Something in her voice alerted Cathal to the fact that there was more to the story there, but he didn't press her. Even if he did want to know what it was that she hid. He didn't want to tell her that he knew her mother and sister were dead, but he wasn't sure how to delicately broach the subject. In the end, he realized there was no good way to ask it.

"Have you asked your mum or sister about any of this?"

As if knowing that was his next question, Sorcha barely blinked as she said, "They're both dead. And before you ask, they died on the same day. At the same time. And I was responsible."

He hadn't expected that. He paused, noting how her statement hadn't been said with anger. There was sorrow, yes, as well as regret. Something else was there, as well. Guilt and shame. He couldn't believe he hadn't noticed them from the very beginning. He should have since he carried the same emotions within him.

"I'm sure that isn't possible," he said. If it had happened, she would now have red eyes. The same rules of the Fae applied, even with Halflings. And especially with one such as she, who had power coming from both her Druid side *and* her Fae side.

Sorcha's gaze lowered to her lap, where she picked at a hangnail on her left thumb. "I assure you, it is. Does that change your opinion of me?"

"No," he answered immediately.

She glanced up at him. "Because you're Dark."

"Because I know that there is always more to a story than one simple statement."

Sorcha smiled, but there was no humor in the action. She kept picking at the nail. "I've not talked about…what happened. Ever. Not even after it happened. Everyone assumed I was in shock. Corann knew, though."

Cathal could well imagine that the previous leader of the Skye

Druids had known a great many things. Cathal remained silent, waiting for her to continue.

"Corann took me aside and stared into my eyes for what felt like an eternity," Sorcha continued after taking a shaky breath. "Then he told Rhona to bring me home. I don't remember the days following that. It's like I blinked and found myself standing by the graves dug into the ground as my mum and sister were lowered into them." She gave a quick bark of laughter. "So many tried to ask me what happened, but Corann quickly silenced them. He remained by my side the entire time, even during the funeral. I thought once everyone left that he would sit me down and ask me what had occurred. But he didn't. He gave me a kiss on the forehead and told me that he'd be there if I needed anything. Then he left."

Cathal swallowed, watching the play of emotions on her face. Her family's deaths might have occurred ten years ago, but to Sorcha, it weighed on her as if it had happened just yesterday.

She lifted her gaze to him. "I didn't leave the house after that. I didn't want to see anyone or talk to anyone. I think everyone believed I was just grieving. Then, as the weeks turned into months, and months into years, they accepted it. Well, everyone except Rhona. She usually comes by every month or so."

"It's good that she does," he said.

Sorcha's lips twisted. "Perhaps. I've long wanted to ask her if Corann told her what happened that day with my family, but I don't have the guts."

"Has Rhona ever treated you differently?"

Sorcha thought about that for a moment before she shook her head.

"Then there's your answer," Cathal told her.

"You've not asked me either."

Cathal glanced at her hands, still picking at the thumb. "Everyone has something in their past they don't want to think about or share with others."

"Including you?"

"Including me. As you've pointed out, I was Dark."

She frowned. "Was?"

"Am," he corrected, wondering why he'd let that slip out.

Her head tilted to the side. "You don't act like a Dark."

"Have you met many of us?" he asked with a grin.

Her lips began to curve slightly. "I can't say that I have. I've only seen one from afar."

"What about the Light Fae?"

She lifted one shoulder in a half-shrug. "They aren't uncommon on Skye."

"That didn't answer my question."

"No, it didn't." She cleared her throat and dropped her chin to her chest. "Mum didn't like Molly or me interacting with the Fae. She didn't care if they were Light or Dark, she wanted us to keep our distance. But Molly and I came across one at the pub one day. I dared her to talk to him, but she wouldn't do it. So, I said I would."

Cathal didn't like the turn this story had taken.

Sorcha glanced up at him. "He was nice. He flirted. I flirted. I was young and stupid, and I honestly believed I could control the situation. We met a couple of times without Molly knowing. We just talked. It was nice."

"I take it that didn't last?" he asked when her eyes got a faraway look in them.

She blinked, coming back to herself. "I think everything changed when I began keeping secrets from my family. We had always shared everything. I know that's unusual, but we had an unusual family. Mum was definitely our parent, but there came a time as we got older that she turned into more of a friend. Not many can say that their mother and sister are their best friends, but that's how it was for me. Every once in a while, we'd convince Mum to go out on a date. She was always being asked out, but there was never a second one. She used to tell us that she'd already found— and lost—her soulmate. I always believed it was her husband."

"But now, after reading the journals, you think it was your father," Cathal guessed.

"I do," she admitted. "Neither Molly nor I asked her for a name. Looking back now, there were several instances we could've pushed her to reveal more."

"You three shared everything. You didn't believe she would keep anything from you."

Sorcha snorted. "I felt so bad for keeping my secrets from her and Molly, and the entire time, Mum had secrets of her own."

"I bet your sister did, as well."

"Probably."

He lowered his foot to the floor. "Just because you know that you're a Halfling and your mum kept that from you doesn't change the fact that the three of you were close and had a great family dynamic."

"And yet, I'm the one who killed them."

"You keep saying that."

"Because it's true."

He drew in a breath. "There is nothing about you that I've seen that would lead me to believe you're a killer."

"Then let me change your mind. One thing we did often was hike and climb. We often freebase climbed, which means without the assistance of ropes. We were that good. Mum had been doing it all her life, and she taught me and Molly. I had been out late the night before, meeting the Light Fae. I was tired, and I didn't want to go climbing. Mum said that we were using the ropes that day because I was cranky. Molly laughed, but Mum was angry. I think she had an idea of what I had been doing. I didn't want her in my business. I thought I was old enough to make my own decisions. I knew that if she began to dig into my affairs, I would move out." Sorcha paused and swallowed.

Cathal watched as she tugged on some of the skin up near her thumbnail. She didn't seem to notice. She was too far into her memories.

"Sure enough, Mum began asking who I had been meeting. I refused to tell her. All I wanted to do was finish with the climb and get back home so I could change and go and meet him again. I was in the lead, with Mum and then Molly behind me. I clipped us in. I heard it. I know I did it."

Cathal couldn't take his eyes from her. She looked straight

ahead, but her gaze was unfocused. Without a doubt, she was living it all over again as she told him the story.

"I wouldn't have been so careless as to risk their lives," Sorcha said in a soft voice. She blinked rapidly for a moment before a tear escaped to drop onto her cheek. She didn't wipe it away as she continued. "I told Mum that it was none of her business and to leave me alone. I was in the process of trying to get a handhold when my fingers slipped. I had a firm grip with my other hand as well as both footholds. I gave my other arm a moment of rest and looked down at my mum and sister. Molly was telling me how selfish I was being as she climbed. Mum was looking up at me, her expression filled with worry. The moment she said my name, I turned away and reached for my next handhold. There was a snap. It was so loud that I hear it in my dreams sometimes."

Cathal slowly sat forward. He needed to get closer to Sorcha, but he didn't want to interrupt her thoughts. Not so much because he wanted to hear the story, but because he wasn't sure what would happen to her if he did.

She swallowed loudly. "Then I felt something pull against the ropes around my waist. Before I could even look down, I heard Molly call for Mum. I didn't panic. Neither did Molly. This wasn't the first time we'd slipped. Mum was calm and patient as she helped Molly find her footing." Sorcha's gaze shifted to him then. "As I looked down at them both, I happened to look over to where I'd clipped us in. The carabiner wasn't locked into place. I realized at that moment that Mum was taking the brunt of the pull from Molly. She was holding it off me so we didn't all fall. I tried to climb down and reclip us, but when I did, it caused Mum to lose her grip. Still, none of us got flustered. To do that is certain death."

Cathal gave her a nod and scooted toward her.

"When Mum lost her grip more, the weight she'd been holding came to me. Any other day, I would've had no problem supporting them both. I'd done it before. But the night before, I'd been out too late, drank too much, and I hadn't slept. I was in no condition to be the lead. I knew everything came down to me holding on, but that awareness seemed to make every muscle in my body shake from exertion. I focused on keeping my foot and toe holds. Molly had never taken so long to get her grips. I didn't realize that when she slipped, she'd cut her finger. Mum managed to lock in place and take some of the weight from me. The last thing I should've done was relax, but I did. I don't even know what happened because I didn't look down. All I know is that Molly screamed. Mum began yelling, telling her to stay calm. I managed to look at them. Mum must have seen that I wouldn't be able to take any more weight. I knew if I didn't do something that they were going to die. So, I did the only thing I could think of. I used magic."

Cathal looked down at her hands to see that she had torn the hangnail off and her finger was bleeding. He rose and went to the other end of the sofa next to her chair and covered her hands with his, using his magic to stop the bleeding.

Sorcha looked at him then. "And it killed them."

CHAPTER ELEVEN

The wave of guilt threatened to drown her, but Sorcha didn't stop it. It's what she deserved. Her mother and sister had counted on her, and she'd let them down.

"I know that isn't true. Because if it was, you'd have red eyes, or you'd be a *drough*. And you're no evil Druid."

The sound of Cathal's deep voice was soothing. She looked up into his face to find him near her. No matter what she did, she couldn't look away from his scarlet eyes. One of his hands covered both of hers. It was large and comforting, just like his voice. Sorcha shook her head. "The magic I used was meant to clip the rope into place and secure us. It didn't. My magic had never missed before.

Mum kept telling me that she had the strength to hold Molly. I knew she did. Even with my sister injured. It should've worked. But everything that could've gone wrong that day did. I could do nothing as Mum's foot slipped, and they both tumbled down to our last hook in. Do you have any idea how it feels to be safe and see your family fall? There was no time for magic, no time for anything. The next moment, they were both dead."

Saying it aloud dredged it all up again. Sorcha had cried so many tears throughout the years, but each time she remembered that day, she cried all over again. She had never felt so helpless or defenseless in her life. She was a Druid from one of the strongest groups in the world. And she hadn't been able to save her family.

"Sometimes bad things happen to good people," Cathal said.

She snorted and lowered her gaze to look at their hands. "If I hadn't been out late the night before, if I hadn't taken the lead, if my magic had worked, if—"

"You could do that for eternity. Whether you want to hear this or not, your mum and sister were there, as well. They hold some of the responsibility. You said yourself that all three of you were experts. I saw you at the cliffs in Ireland. I can tell how good you are. I may not have known your mother, but she doesn't sound like the type of woman who would've let you take the lead if she didn't think you could handle it."

Sorcha shrugged. "It was a climb we'd made many times."

"Accidents happen. That doesn't mean you're to blame just because you survived."

"I wish I could believe you, but I was there. I witnessed all of it."

He licked his lips and briefly lowered his gaze. "Had your sister ever cut her finger before on a climb?"

"No, but I have. It makes it impossible to climb."

"You couldn't have possibly known that she'd do that."

Sorcha smiled. "I know what you're doing, but the simple fact is, if I'd made sure we were clipped in, none of that would have happened."

"You can't know that for sure."

"Neither can you. I didn't take the climb seriously. It was one of the rules my mother had. None of us climbed unless our heads were completely in it. You had to have total concentration, or you could fall."

His nostrils flared as he held his gaze. "It sounds like none of you had full concentration that day if you were arguing."

Sorcha parted her lips to respond when she realized that he was right. "That doesn't take away my culpability, however."

"It was a tragedy to be sure. You hate the Fae because had you not been talking with one, you wouldn't have stayed out or kept secrets from your family," Cathal pointed out. "You don't do magic because you feel like it let you down when you needed it the most. You don't leave the house because you don't feel as if you should be living while your family is gone. And you don't want to be a part of anything to do with the Druids because you think you don't deserve it."

She narrowed her eyes at him. "You got all of that by my story?"

"No," he said softly. "I got all of that by watching you, hearing the story, and feeling your emotions."

Sorcha looked away, feeling more vulnerable and exposed than she had in a very long time. She hadn't told a single person that story. Not Corann, not her friends, not the authorities. No one. When the police asked her questions, it was just to confirm that it had been an accident. She'd wanted to tell them the truth, but she hadn't been able to get the words out.

Cathal blinked, his forehead furrowing. "Bloody hell. You think the authorities should've locked you away."

"How do you do that?" she asked. "I said nothing aloud."

"It's all over your face."

Sorcha shrugged. "It's true. I do feel like I should be in jail. Everything you said before was right. Except I would add that I should be behind bars, not living my life."

"You didn't kill your mother and sister," Cathal stated firmly. "Corann must have known that as well, or he wouldn't have stayed by your side."

Now it was her turn to frown. "You knew Corann?"

"I didn't know him personally, but I knew of him."

"Who are you?" Because one thing was for certain, he wasn't like anyone she'd ever met before.

Cathal couldn't hold her gaze. "You know who I am."

"No, I don't, actually. You're a Fae with a Dark's coloring, but you don't act like any Dark I've heard about. You just seem…different."

"Because I am."

"I opened up to you and told you my deepest, darkest secret, and you can't even tell me who you are?" Sorcha pulled her hands from his and got to her feet. She walked away from him a few paces before she stopped and looked back. "I've told you things I've never shared before. Not because you forced me but because I wanted to. You're the first stranger that has been inside this house in years. You sought me out. Why? Just to tell me I'm a Halfling? Why does it matter what's in my blood?"

Cathal slowly got to his feet. "Because you're in danger."

"From some Fae wanting to sleep with me to get me pregnant?" She laughed and quirked a brow. "That wouldn't happen to be you, would it? I mean, if I was ever going to take a Fae to my bed, I have to admit, you definitely fit the bill."

To her shock, he seemed unable to find words.

"Is that it?" she pressed. "You saving me in Ireland, you rescuing me from the Light Fae at the pools, and then coming here and healing my ankle. Was it all a setup for you to get into my pants?"

"No," he said with a shake of his head.

She shrugged and let her arms fall to her sides. "I'll be honest, it's been a very, very long time since I've had sex. I might have forgotten how to do it, actually. But at the end of the day, I'm not interested in anything like that. Not with anyone. Even you, as hot as you are. And the very last thing I want is to get pregnant."

"Then you better do the ritual."

Sorcha rolled her eyes and walked to the door. "Thank you for the information. I'll consider it, but I think it's time you left."

At that exact moment, there was a knock on the door, followed by a woman's Irish voice. "Cathal, you need to get out here!"

"What the hell?" Sorcha asked as she gaped at Cathal. "Did you think I was into threesomes? Just when I thought things couldn't get any weirder."

Cathal strode past her. "This is nothing sexual. The Fae are surrounding your house, vying to get to you. The moment you leave for anything, they'll pounce on you like that Light Fae did today. And no, whatever you may think of me, I haven't done any of this just to get into your pants. As appealing as that may sound."

Sorcha was so shocked at his words that she could only look at him as he removed her hand and opened the door. Then she found herself staring at a gorgeous Dark Fae female with long, black and silver hair that was done up in numerous small braids. Her red eyes landed on Sorcha before she beckoned to Cathal with a long, red nail.

"Things are getting pretty intense out here, big guy," the woman said.

Cathal looked at Sorcha. "No matter what happens, stay inside the house. You're protected in here."

Before she could even nod, he shut the door as he walked out. Sorcha rushed to the window and jerked open the curtains, but there was no sign of either of them. She blinked before running to another window, then another, and another, and another. It didn't matter where she looked, she couldn't see Cathal or the woman. She didn't have any lights outside the house, but the moon was nearly full and shed enough light on the land to make it easy to see. Sorcha was turning away when she saw something along the fence that separated her property from her neighbor. There was a man there. Just standing. Not far from him was another figure.

She jerked back and quickly snapped the curtains closed, utterly unnerved. Sorcha looked around the cottage to find all the drapes open. She hastily shut them and then went back to her chair and wrapped her arms around herself.

Her ears strained to hear anything, but only silence met her. Everything Cathal had told her came back to her in stereo. She couldn't stop thinking about the men she'd seen along the fence. Were they the Fae Cathal had said were coming to impregnate her?

If they were, she had a feeling they wouldn't care if they forced her or not.

The notion caused a chill to race down her back. It was one thing to think Cathal had come to woo her to have sex, and quite another to imagine some Fae raping her. And all she had to do was think about the Light Fae at the Fairy Pools. He simply hadn't wanted to take no for an answer. If Cathal hadn't been there…

"And I just blew him off," she said with a shake of her head. She couldn't believe he had actually found her house and tried to talk to her again.

If it had been Sorcha, and she'd been treated the way she had done with Cathal, she would've gone the other way. It just proved once more that the Fae didn't act anything like how she'd thought a Dark should act. Then again, all she had to go on was what she'd been told about the Dark Fae—that they were evil.

And the red eyes, along with the silver in the hair, pretty much made that easy to spot.

Droughs, however, weren't so easy to distinguish from the *mie*. Sometimes, a Druid didn't know until it was too late. With the Fae, they could use glamour to hide their true colors, so to speak. But she didn't think Cathal used glamour with her. In fact, he'd said that he should have used it so she didn't see his Dark coloring.

Why had he shown her who he was? Was it because he wanted to see how she reacted? Or was it because he didn't care?

Minutes crawled by as she stared at the door, wondering and waiting to see what was going on outside with Cathal, the Dark female, and whoever else was out there. The woman had made it seem as if there were others that needed to be dealt with. Even Sorcha had seen the men along the fence. Is that who the woman had been talking about?

Sorcha had started to nod off when something made her open her eyes to find Cathal and the woman standing in her living room. Cathal's shirt was torn, giving her a glimpse of his chiseled abs. He was breathing hard, and his long hair had come loose from its queue. Sweat soaked his shirt and lined his brow. The woman held her side as she clenched her teeth together. Her face was smudged with mud, and her black clothing was smeared with grass and dirt.

Sorcha jumped to her feet. "What happened?"

"We took care of the fekkers," the woman said. Then she grimaced. "Sorry. I'm Aisling, by the way."

Sorcha looked from Cathal to Aisling. "Hi."

"They're gone for now, but they'll be back," Cathal said.

Aisling pulled her hand away from her side to reveal a wound. After looking at it briefly, she said, "I hope so. Tonight was fun."

Cathal grunted, but his gaze was on Sorcha.

"Are you hurt?" she asked him.

Aisling answered. "We heal. Don't worry about us."

"Oh," Sorcha said, hating to miss an excuse to touch Cathal's fine body once more. Then she frowned. "How did you two get in?"

Cathal shrugged one shoulder. "We're Fae."

"But if you can get in, can't the others?" she asked.

Aisling's red eyes snapped to Cathal. "Did you not tell her?"

"I hadn't gotten to that part yet," he said as he turned his head to Aisling.

Sorcha raised her brows. "Perhaps now would be a good time."

"They want you," Aisling said. "And they'll do anything to get to you. As far as we can see, there is only one old ward on the property to keep the Fae out. It's weathered and worn. We're not sure how much longer it'll hold."

Sorcha didn't miss the fact that Aisling had said it would keep the Fae out. If both she and Cathal were Fae—and they certainly looked Fae—then how did they get in? Sorcha kept that tidbit to herself for the moment. It wasn't the first time that something like this had been said. After all, Cathal had mentioned that he'd once *been* Dark. As if he weren't anymore.

"So, what do we do now?" Sorcha asked.

Cathal shook his head as he looked at Aisling. "We should be fine tonight. It's tomorrow I'm worried about."

"They'll be back soon, and probably with more numbers," Aisling added. "We should probably get a few more to help us."

Cathal's lips twisted. "I'm not sure that's an option."

"I'm pretty sure it is," Aisling replied.

Sorcha didn't like feeling as if they kept secrets from her. There was definitely something going on, but she couldn't put her finger on it. Besides, she was still wrapped up in learning that she was a Halfling, finding out that her mother had many secrets, and remembering what had happened to her family. It was almost too much for her to take in.

Add to that was the fact that she'd just learned some Fae wanted to put their seed inside her… Yeah, she teetered on the edge of fuckery the likes of which she'd never experienced before.

"What if I went somewhere more secure?" Sorcha asked.

Two pairs of red eyes swung her way. Cathal was the first to speak. "We just need to keep you guarded until the ritual."

"That is if you want to do the ritual," Aisling said.

Cathal's face lined with anger as he glared at the Dark. "Of course, she wants to do the ritual. It's the answer to everything."

"Is it?" Sorcha asked. She looked between the two. "I've not done the ritual in ten years. This is the first time I've been approached by Fae—any Fae. It's too much of a coincidence. It has to be more than the family ritual. My mother never missed a ritual."

Aisling's eyes narrowed slightly. "Are you sure about that?"

"It's what she told me," Sorcha said. Then she realized that her mother had left out a lot of things about her past, including who Sorcha's father was. "I…well, to be honest, I don't know anymore, really."

Aisling shrugged. "There's one way to find out if it is the ritual or something else."

"No," Cathal snapped, his brows drawn together, waves of ire rolling off him.

Sorcha ignored Cathal and stared at Aisling. "And what is your suggestion?"

"Aisling, no," Cathal said in a low, dangerous voice.

The Dark raised a black brow and returned his scowl with one of her own. "She's a grown woman and has the right to choose. And she's right. If you'd put aside your feelings and look at the facts, you'd see it, too. No Fae have bothered her in *ten years*. That's ten years of not doing the ritual. Why now? What was it that brought all the Fae to Skye for her?"

Sorcha watched as a muscle twitched in Cathal's jaw. After several tense moments, he turned his head to Sorcha. "As much as I hate to admit it, you are an adult. You can make your own decisions."

The fact that he worried for her was obvious—and something Sorcha felt deeply. From the first moment she'd met Cathal, he had affected her. She'd let him in when she had turned everyone else away. She still wasn't sure why that was, and it didn't matter right now. The important thing was that he and Aisling wanted to keep her safe from everyone else.

She drew in a deep breath and released it as she held Cathal's gaze. "I want to know the real reason the Fae are after me. However, I won't make things more difficult for you in the process. So, what would you suggest I do?"

CHAPTER TWELVE

Cathal couldn't believe that Sorcha had asked for his advice. He was so shocked, he could only stand there.

"Well, look at that," Aisling said in a low voice so that only he could hear.

There was a smile in her quip, but he ignored it. He couldn't take his eyes off Sorcha. No one had ever put their lives in his hands before. It was both exhilarating and terrifying. If he messed up even the tiniest bit, it could mean her life. The responsibility was debilitating.

Why it had been okay when he was guarding her before, he wasn't sure. Something about her saying the words altered…

everything. He couldn't tell her that, though. Instead, he began to think of anything that could keep her from being attacked by Fae hell-bent on forcing themselves on her.

"Cathal?"

Fek. Even the sound of his name on her lips with her slight Scottish brogue was enough to make his balls tighten. He was in way over his head. He'd probably been that way from the very beginning, but he'd been too enamored by her to realize it. But now that it was before him as huge as the moon with bright red blinking lights, he couldn't forget it.

"He's thinking," Aisling said for him.

Cathal swallowed, or at least he attempted to. There was no moisture in his mouth. It was as dry as the Sahara. They needed reinforcements. All of the Reapers needed to be here. But would that even be enough? He needed to get Erith and Cael here, as well.

He suddenly grunted as a small, narrow elbow jabbed him in the ribs. He glanced over to see Aisling giving him a look filled with daggers. Cathal blinked, then looked at Sorcha to find the Halfling giving him a worried look. Fek, but he had to get his shite together. And quickly.

"I don't think leaving is a possibility," he said. "This place has kept the Fae out. They've yet to cross onto your property, and all we can do is hope that holds out until it's time for the ritual."

Sorcha tucked a piece of hair behind her right ear. "And if it doesn't?"

"Then we kick some arse," Aisling said with a wide grin.

Cathal shot her an annoyed look and directed his attention back to Sorcha. "Then we'll take you someplace safe."

"Why not do that now?" Sorcha asked. "I don't want to do the ritual. I told you already. I don't want anything to do with magic."

Aisling released a loud, drawn-out sigh. "Look, Sorcha, I'm going to tell you like it is. Sure, you've been lucky, and no Fae have come before now. Let's say you don't do the ritual this year. What are you going to do when the Fae return next year? Or the year after that? How long do you think you can go before they find you and get what they want? We won't always be around to save your arse."

"I'm not asking you to do it now," the Halfling retorted.

Instead of getting angry, Aisling smiled. "I like you. A lot. You've got steel for a spine, even in a situation where most would be crying in a corner." The Reaper let the smile die. "We've gone to a lot of trouble to keep you alive. Don't repay us by being stupid."

Cathal slid his gaze back to Sorcha. She stared at Aisling for a full minute without saying a word. He wasn't sure what was going on, and he was prepared for anything. After all, Aisling was never shy about telling people the truth.

"You're right. I am being stupid." Sorcha shrugged. "I don't mean to make either of you feel as if I don't appreciate what you're doing. I do. But I'm not going to do magic. No one and nothing can make me change my mind. And being a part of the ritual means I'd have to do magic."

Cathal nodded as he met Sorcha's gaze. "Then we come up with a plan where you don't have to."

"Guess I'm in," Aisling said with a twist of her lips.

Sorcha smiled, and it hit Cathal right in the gut. Her emerald eyes crinkled at the corners, bright with happiness and trust. He'd never felt so inadequate for a mission before. He'd also never been so drawn to another. That played into it, it had to. What other reason could he have for reacting in such a way?

Aisling rolled her eyes as she shook her head. "First, we need to strengthen the ward around the property. I can't believe just one old ward has held the Fae off all these years."

"Good idea," Cathal said. His eyes dropped to Sorcha's mouth. He wanted a taste of it. Hell, he wanted to taste all of her.

Aisling cleared her throat loudly. "That might hold them off for now. And perhaps next year. But after that? I don't know. They may not wait for this time of year. They may come after her every day. The minute she leaves the property, they'll make a move."

"I won't leave," Sorcha stated.

Cathal blinked, taken aback. "You intend to spend the rest of your life in this house? You ventured out today. You liked it. I saw that."

Sorcha shrugged. "You know why I'll stay here. Besides, they won't want me all my life. Just during my childbearing years."

"You're killing me," Aisling said as she turned and walked to the sofa before she sat down and crossed one leg over the other.

Cathal took a step closer to Sorcha. "I understand why you're doing this, but you need to think about yourself. You don't want to do magic, that's fine. But the Fae don't care. They just want what you can give them, and they'll take it any way they can. You'll drop your guard one day, and then they'll have you."

"What would you have me do?" Sorcha asked. "The ritual? Bow down to what everyone wants me to do?"

Aisling lifted a hand. "I'd like to point out that the Fae don't want you to do the ritual. That's why they're here. Because you've not done it."

"I'm still not buying that. They're here for another reason," Sorcha said.

Cathal had to admit that he had begun to wonder that himself. He turned and looked at Aisling. Their gazes met, and she blew out an exasperated breath as she got to her feet.

"You want us to dig deeper into that theory?" the Dark asked.

Cathal nodded as he glanced at Sorcha. "You can stay here and finish healing. I'll see what I can find."

"Oh, no. I'm good to go," Aisling said before she disappeared.

Sorcha's head jerked to him. "What did she just do?"

"Teleported. We also call it jumping."

"Can you do that?"

"Aye. Most Fae can after they achieve a certain amount of power through their magic," he explained.

Sorcha looked at her door and then back at him. "That's how the two of you got in here."

"It is."

"I guess that makes traveling easy. I always thought the Fae had to use doorways like we have at the Fairy Pools."

He shrugged. "Some Fae don't have a choice but to use doorways."

"And you're Fae?" she asked with raised brows.

Cathal frowned. "Of course."

"Tell me again why you're helping me?"

"Because you need it."

She gave him an odd look. "Do you always go around helping Halflings?"

"Not usually."

"Then why me?"

Damn, his words were getting tangled. "Because you needed it."

"You said that already."

Cathal dropped his chin to his chest and sighed. Then he looked at her. "The truth is, I can't tell you what you want to know. Not all of it, at least. I'm a friend. If you believe nothing else, believe that."

"I do believe that." She gave him a soft smile. "Thank you for all of this. I know I'm not making it easy."

"We'll figure it out. In the meantime, either Aisling or I will be here to guard you."

She wrapped her arms around herself. "I'm glad I met you."

Cathal wanted to look away. He needed to look away from Sorcha. Yet he was powerless to do anything but sink further into the emerald depths of her eyes. Did she know the pull she had over him? Did she realize how badly he ached for her? His hands still tingled from carrying her in Ireland, from feeling her soft body against his. The way her arms had wrapped around him had him craving her with a hunger that would never be quenched.

Her arms slowly dropped to her sides, and she took a step toward him. Cathal felt the tug to her. He was so tired of resisting it, of ignoring it, that he gave in. The minute he moved in her direction, Sorcha rushed to him. His arms came around her instantly as their lips met.

The feel of her was everything he'd thought it would be and more. Her hands tangled in his hair. He groaned as her nails softly scraped his scalp. His tongue slid along the seam of her lips. Her mouth parted, and he slipped his tongue inside to duel with hers.

The kiss rocked him to his very core. The taste of her was captivating, electrifying. And with one kiss, he knew he had to have more. Unable to resist, he deepened the kiss. She sank against him. He wrapped his arms around her tighter, holding her up as he plundered her lips.

Suddenly, Sorcha ended the kiss and pulled away from him. He made his arms release her, directed himself to let her go even as every fiber of his being bellowed to have her back against him. No one had ever affected him in such a way. He'd felt desire, he'd experienced lust. Whatever this thing was with Sorcha was deeper, stronger than anything he'd experienced before.

He knew the best thing to do would be for him to turn around and forget all about the soul-stirring kiss they'd just shared. But he didn't. He didn't have the will to do anything but stay with her.

She hesitantly touched her lips that were now swollen from his kisses. At the base of her throat, he saw the erratic beat of her heart. She was just as affected as he was. The difference was that she'd had the strength to pull away. If only he had the same. There was no room in his life for someone. It didn't matter if other Reapers had found love. Cathal had never wanted anyone. He'd been content on his own, giving his life to the Reapers and Death. It was all he'd signed up for.

This…whatever *this* was…couldn't continue.

Even as he made up his mind, his heart laughed. He wanted Sorcha. Wanted her as he'd never wanted another thing before. Not even revenge. When he was with her, he didn't feel the baggage of his past. He forgot that he'd been Dark. He forgot…everything but her.

"I've wanted to kiss you since that first night I saw you in that storm in Ireland," he told her.

She smiled shyly and lowered her arm. "I couldn't stop thinking about you."

There was so much he wanted to tell her, but he'd never been good with words. They always got tangled up in his mind. He was better in battle, where he'd been used most of his life. Yet he found he wanted to be something different with Sorcha. He wanted to be able to voice the feelings within him.

His lips parted, but all the words evaporated. Then he realized he didn't need words. He could show her. Cathal held out his hand. Sorcha slowly reached out and took it. He then tugged her toward him, back into his arms where she had been. He gazed down at her, marveling at her beauty.

He traced the pads of his fingers down her face to her neck. Then he slid his hand around to her nape and held her. Slowly, he lowered his head and brushed his lips against hers. The moment their lips met, the flames of desire flared higher than before. She rose up on her tiptoes and wound her arms around his neck. Then, she sighed.

The sound went straight to his hard cock, making it jump. Their attraction was too intense, too forceful to be denied. He backed her up until he had her pinned against a wall. Then he slid his hands down around the backs of her thighs. He lifted her, and instinctively, her legs wrapped around his waist.

She tore her mouth from his, gasping for air as he kissed down her throat. He rocked his arousal against her, wringing another moan from Sorcha. Cathal was so far gone that the house could be burning down around them and he wouldn't know.

CHAPTER THIRTEEN

Breathe. She needed to breathe.

But everything felt so good. Sorcha's body was on fire, and it was all because of Cathal. The way he held her, the way he kissed her, the way he touched her. She still couldn't believe they had kissed. She'd been standing there thinking how fortunate she was that he'd come into her life, and how goddamn beautiful he was. The next thing she knew, she was in his arms.

And she didn't regret a single second of it.

Their ragged breaths filled her ears while her blood heated in her veins. When Cathal ground his arousal against her, she groaned, wishing he was closer. His kisses curled her toes and made her weak in the knees. All she could think about was having him inside her, of feeling him move against her.

She tried to tell him what she wanted, but she couldn't think while he touched her. Between his mouth and hands, she could barely string a thought together. Finally, she gave up and yanked at his shirt. He must have understood because the next thing she knew, the shirt was gone. Except it wasn't just his shirt. It was all of his clothes.

Sorcha pushed him away until she stood on her feet once more. She saw his frown, and knew she should tell him that she didn't want him to stop, but she couldn't manage it. Instead, she stared in awe at the man before her. He was…perfection. A work of art. She couldn't understand why anyone with that kind of body would keep it hidden beneath clothes.

"Holy shit," she murmured and pushed away from the wall.

Only a few inches separated them, but it was far too many. Sorcha put her hands on his chest and marveled at the thick muscles beneath her palms. There wasn't an inch of fat on him anywhere. Every muscle was shaped to perfection.

Slowly, she ran her hands down his chest to his washboard stomach and then back up again to smooth over his broad shoulders then down the hard sinew of his arms. She couldn't stop touching him. As she made her way back down his stomach, she kept going. She moved over his hips to his tight ass, then around to the front. She purposefully didn't touch his cock.

When she glanced up at his face, his neck was corded, and his eyes were shut as if it pained him to remain still as she enjoyed her perusal of his amazing body. She hadn't asked him to stay still, but once more, he had proven that he knew exactly what she wanted. It was definitely something she could get used to.

Sorcha didn't want to think of the future. She wanted to keep focused on the present moment and what was before her. A stunning man, who made her feel like she was alive again. A Fae who brought out her desire and forced her to surrender to it.

With her gaze locked on his face, she reached between them and wrapped her fingers around his length. Instantly, his eyes flew open and pinned her. In his crimson gaze, she saw his desire, his need. His…hunger.

Her heart skipped a beat. She might have shut herself away from the world, but even she knew this was something special, something not to be ignored. She didn't deserve this, but she was going to take it anyway. One night. That's all she wanted. One night with a man who was everything she hadn't known she wanted.

Or needed.

She used her free hand and reached for the button of her jeans. Cathal placed his hand over hers. In a blink, her clothes were gone. They never broke eye contact as he moved her hair away from her face. She stroked him slowly, moving her hand up and down his shaft.

"You've no idea how beautiful you are," he told her. "Or how much I hunger for you."

His words had been unexpected and touched her deeply. She didn't know what to say to such a compliment, so she rose up on her toes and placed her lips against his. Then she released his cock and took his hand as she led him down the hall to her bedroom.

He turned her when they got to the bed and put a knee on the mattress before he lifted her and gently laid her down. She reached for him, but he smiled and pinned her hands over her head. Sorcha should have expected that he would make her remain still so he could look at her as she had with him.

Her stomach trembled with excitement as heat smoldered in his gaze. He placed a quick kiss on her lips before he straightened and stared down at her.

Nothing could ever compare to the sight of Sorcha naked. Cathal accepted this fact easily. He gazed down at the Halfling lying seductively on the bed and was awed, utterly overcome with emotion. Her pale skin shone blue in the moonlight coming through the slit in the curtains. Her breasts were large enough to fill his palms. Her pink-tipped nipples were hard, waiting for his touch.

His gaze traveled down the indent of her waist to the flare of her hips. Then he paused to admire the junction of her thighs. The auburn curls there were neatly trimmed and glistening with her arousal. Her long legs brushed against each other before she opened for him. The sight of her sex made his cock jump, eager to be surrounded by her wet heat.

Now that he had seen her, it was his time to touch her. Cathal stretched out beside her. With his free hand, he traced a line from her rapidly beating pulse down between her breasts before circling back to make a circuit around each delicate mound. Only then did he lean over and wrap his mouth around a turgid nipple.

Her back arched as she sucked in a breath. Cathal smiled inwardly because he was just getting started.

There was no way she'd last much longer. Sorcha was already teetering on the brink of an orgasm, and all Cathal had done was suckle her nipple.

All thought ceased when his hand found her neglected peak and began to tease it. That, along with the pull from his mouth on her other breast, had her gripping the comforter as the pleasure poured mercilessly through her.

As suddenly as it began, it ended. Sorcha took a moment and tried to catch her breath. As soon as she relaxed, he moved and settled himself between her legs. She barely had time to register that before his mouth was on her sex. His tongue was soft as it licked her then began to swirl around her clit.

That's all it took for the climax to claim her. She jerked from the force of it, a scream locked in her throat. Cathal never stopped licking her. The faster his tongue laved, the more intense the orgasm became. It seemed to go on forever, wringing her of everything.

When she was finally able to open her eyes again, she realized that he had traded his hand for his mouth. In and out, his finger plunged, stroking her slowly, setting up a rhythm that she found herself rocking her hips in tempo with. To her shock, it didn't take long for her body to begin building toward another climax.

But she wanted him inside her. She wanted to feel his length, to have him stretch her. To experience his weight atop her.

"I need you," she told him.

He looked into her eyes and gave a nod. As he shifted over her, Sorcha reached for his cock and stroked his hard length several times before guiding it into her body. The feel of the blunt head of his arousal made her hold her breath in anticipation. And with one thrust, he was seated inside her.

She clutched him, her body sighing with contentment. When he began to move, she closed her eyes and gave herself to the pleasure.

He was ruined for anyone else. Cathal knew and accepted the fact easily. Sorcha fit him to perfection. She was a sight to behold as she climaxed. The ecstasy on her face had humbled him and made him want to pleasure her again and again and again.

Now that he was inside her, he knew true contentment. Her wet heat wrapped around him tightly. He began to move gradually, not wanting to hurt her. Then she locked her ankles around his waist. It was all he needed to begin rocking his hips. He thrust hard and deep, tumbling himself headlong into the type of pleasure that changed a man completely.

He ground his teeth together, wanting to give her another orgasm before he gave in to his own. The moment he felt her body tense, he knew it was too late for him. The climax was swift, engulfing him in decadence that promised more delight than he had any right to.

When he finally came back to himself once more, he felt Sorcha lightly running her hands up and down his back. He rose up and looked at her. She smiled at him and smoothed his hair away from his face. Once more, he wanted to share his feelings with her, but he didn't even try to find the words.

Instead, he pulled out of her and rolled onto his back, taking her with him. Her smile was still in place as she rested her cheek against his pec. He stared at the ceiling, still marveling at the bliss he'd just experienced. He hadn't known anything like that existed. If he had, he'd have been searching for it all this time.

But now that he'd found it? Cathal wasn't sure… Sorcha was a Halfling, and he was a Reaper. If she wouldn't do magic to save herself, he couldn't imagine that she would ever leave her home to be with him.

He let the moment pass without sharing his feelings, and knew that was probably for the best. They'd shared their bodies, and while the sex had been amazing, he didn't want to ruin it by telling Sorcha that he was falling hard for her.

CHAPTER FOURTEEN

Without a doubt, she was falling for Cathal. Sorcha had known in the back of her mind that giving in to the desire would put her on such a path. But she hadn't been able to say no. And she was glad she hadn't. Even now, her body hummed with relaxation and satisfaction like never before.

It felt nice to be held against him. In fact, it felt as close to perfection as anything she had imagined. And she had fantasized about quite a lot of things over the past decade. What it would be like to fall in love, to get married, to have children, to grow old with someone. She'd also thought about divorce, never finding anyone, and living alone.

In all her imaginings, meeting a man like Cathal had never popped into her mind. Mainly because she'd never factored the Fae into anything. It was still difficult for her to accept that she was part Fae. She couldn't understand why her mother hadn't told her. Why was it such a secret?

Cathal's slowly wound one of her curls around his finger. She smiled because no one had ever played with her hair. And it felt so good.

"You can do that forever," she told him.

He chuckled. "I gather you like it."

"I can't begin to tell you how wonderful it feels."

"Better than sex?"

She thought about that a moment. "Not better, different."

"I was beginning to wonder if you'd answer."

They shared a laugh. Then, she shifted her head to look at him. "The sex was incredible."

"Yes, it was," he said as his red eyes met hers.

She bit her lip. "Although, it's probably because I've not had sex with anyone for ten years." Sorcha cut her eyes to him, barely able to hold back her smile.

Cathal flipped her onto her back and held himself over her with his arms all the while smiling. "Tease."

"Sorry. I couldn't help it." She wiped the smile away and touched his face reverently. "I wasn't lying. What you did to me was marvelous, wonderful, astounding—"

"Thank you," he said, cutting her off. He lowered his head to place a soft kiss to her lips. "I can honestly say that I've never felt anything like what we shared tonight."

Before she could think of something to say, he returned to lying on his back. She rolled with him, resuming her spot. "Are you all right? You don't regret it, do you?"

"No," he answered quickly. His arms came around her, holding her tightly. "Never."

"What happens now?"

"I have no idea. You?"

She shook her head. "Not a clue. I guess we'll play it by ear."

"Sure."

But that didn't sound like something he wanted to do. The problem was that she didn't know *what* to do. She hadn't dated in ages, and she wasn't even sure if what they were doing was dating or just having sex. The adult thing to do would be to discuss it. That was if he wanted to have that conversation. For all she knew, this was his way of stopping any kind of talk before it got started.

The heady feeling from before began to fade. Sorcha tried to hold onto it. This had the best thing to happen to her in years. A wee bit of guilt tried to worm its way in, but she stopped it before it could. She didn't think about why she did it either.

"This may not be the proper time to talk, but if you want to find out why the Fae are suddenly here for you, then we'll come up with a plan."

She was so shocked by his words that, for a moment, she didn't move. "I would like that. I'm not sure how to do it, or even if it would work, but it's just all so strange."

"The more I think about it, the more I agree with you. Why now? And you're sure you've never seen any Fae before near your property?"

"Never. I do walk outside and tend to the gardens. I interact with the horses from the neighbor to my right and sometimes feed the baby cows. I leave the house. I just don't normally leave the property," she explained.

He drew in a breath. "What about at night?"

"I often sit outside by the firepit and look at the stars. Trust me, I would've noticed if someone was watching me."

"That's what I thought." Cathal rubbed his hand up and down her back. "What you want to do will be dangerous."

She lifted her head and rose up on her elbow to look at him. "I'm prepared for that. I did scale the side of a cliff in a storm not too long ago."

His red eyes held hers. "This will be different. The Fae will say and do anything to get you to go with them. You won't be able to believe anything they say. I don't care what coloring they show you. You can't trust any of it or them."

"I trust you."

"You've no idea how much that means to me." He reached up and touched her face before tucking her hair behind her ear.

Sorcha licked her lips and studied Cathal. "You mentioned that you were once Dark, as if you aren't now. Both you and Aisling kept saying the ward on my property would keep Fae out, but it didn't stop either of you. Even if I ask, you won't tell me what you are, will you?"

He slowly shook his head, regret filling his face.

"It's all right," she told him and kissed him. Then she lay back on his chest. "You once told me that everyone has secrets. You're right. Everyone does. And no one has a right to ask what they are."

"But you told me yours."

She released a breath. "That was my decision. I won't be angry at you if you never tell me yours. Sometimes, it's better if secrets are never shared. There is a reason they're called secrets." Then, before he could reply, she said, "If we confront any of the Fae to find out what they really want, is there any way you can hide nearby?"

"Of course."

She lay back on his chest. "That makes me feel better. I don't want to put you and Aisling in any kind of danger."

"You don't need to worry about us. Ever. We'll be fine."

"I saw the two of you earlier after your fights with the Fae outside."

He made a sound in the back of his throat. "That was nothing."

The more he talked, the more she began to realize there was a lot about Cathal she didn't know. And maybe it was better that way. When everything was said and done, he'd be gone and out of her life. Just thinking about everything that had to line up for them to meet boggled her mind. Then there was the fact that she didn't deserve to find any kind of happiness.

She had accepted her life and her Fate long ago. Just because Cathal was here now, and she was enjoying herself, didn't mean that it was forever. That thought sobered her, wiping away any vestiges of bliss that still lingered. This time when she looked to the future, it was bleak and miserable. There was no way she could get through the days as she had been for the last decade. Not when everywhere she looked, she saw Cathal.

Was that what had happened to her mum? Had she seen her husband everywhere after he died? And what of her Fae lover? If her mother had suffered, she'd never let it show. Not once. Even when Sorcha and Molly prodded her to date. Her mum continued saying that she didn't need anyone in her life.

Sorcha had believed it was because there was no one out there who matched her mother. After all, it had been years and years since her husband had died. Surely, her mum would've gotten over him by then. Now, Sorcha had begun to think it was because her mother's heart had been taken. She had fallen in love, the kind that lasts lifetimes. When her mother couldn't have her lover, she had given up any thoughts and hopes of finding happiness with someone else. She'd been content to spend her days with her daughters.

The awareness of that hit Sorcha like a freight train. She struggled for breath, trying to get enough oxygen into her lungs, even as her mind bellowed at the truth. She closed her eyes, refusing to cry any more tears.

Cathal's arms tightened around her. He didn't ask what was wrong, didn't prod into her thoughts. He simply held her, which was precisely what she needed. Sorcha didn't know how many minutes passed before she could breathe normally again. All she knew was that if she hadn't met Cathal, if she hadn't shared her body with him, she wouldn't have any idea what her mum had gone through. She wouldn't have any inkling about the silent pain her mother had hidden from everyone.

All these years after her mother's and sister's deaths, Sorcha still carried her grief around for everyone to see. Her mother had been the strong one. It took courage and resilience and determination to know that the man she'd given her heart to would never return. And that their love would have to remain a secret.

Cathal's hand smoothed her hair back from her face as he kissed her brow. She sniffed, overcome with emotions. The day had been draining. First, she had gone to the cove, then the Fairy Pools. She'd discovered that she was a Halfling, read her mother's journals, and uncovered many secrets. She'd learned that the Fae were after her to plant their seed within her, and then she had slept with Cathal.

"Have you ever looked back at the past and realized that you were wrong—about so very much?" she asked him.

He released a breath. "I have. It's not an easy thing to accept."

"I wouldn't have been able to do it without you."

He stilled for an instant. "I don't understand."

"I thought my mum wanted to be on her own without a man. I thought she had gotten over the death of her husband and just couldn't find a man who could match her." Sorcha looked at Cathal. "All those years, she hid her grief, despair, and loneliness. I never had any sort of hint to any of it. She did it for me and for Molly."

"Because she loved you both."

Sorcha glanced away. "I've let everyone know I'm suffering for what happened. Mum didn't. She put a smile on her face and waited until she was alone before she let her true emotions show. She was so strong."

Cathal turned onto his side to face her. "So are you."

"Thank you for saying that, but I'm not even close."

"You climbed a cliff face in a storm to spy on Druids. You want to face the Fae after you. You're no slouch in the courage department."

His words made her smile. "I'm glad you found me. I'm glad you told me about my heritage. It's opened my eyes to so many things. Thank you."

"I should be the one thanking you. No one has put their lives in my hands before."

"I find that hard to believe. Look at everything you've done for me."

He lifted one shoulder as his gaze darted away briefly. "My interactions aren't usually with Halflings or mortals. Only Fae."

"And yet, you spoke with me."

"I couldn't help myself."

Her grin widened. "You've changed my life."

"You've changed mine, as well."

"You're a Fae. How in the world could I do that? I'm only a Halfling, who didn't even realize that until today."

His gaze was intense, solemn. "You discount yourself. I've come across a great many people in my life, and you surpass all of them. You have no idea how special you are."

His words touched her. If only she could tell him that she wanted to be special to him. But she couldn't get the sentiment past her lips. It was partly because she still believed she should be punished for the deaths of her mother and sister, but another part knew that she didn't belong in Cathal's world.

And he didn't belong in hers.

Why then did she wish so much that they could be together?

She reached for his hand, and their fingers twined together. They said nothing, just stared into each other's eyes, both lost in thought. She didn't think of the past or the future. Instead, she put every second they had together to memory so she could look back on it later, all the while, opening herself to him completely.

Then, Cathal swallowed and wound one of her curls around his finger again. "I didn't lie to you before. I was Dark, but my family raised me as a Light."

Now that surprised her. "How did they take you becoming Dark?"

"My mother died when I was very young. For a while, it was just my dad and me. Then he met someone and remarried. She had a daughter from a previous marriage, and then they had two children together. Two more girls."

Sorcha watched him carefully. She didn't know why he was telling her this, but she was glad that he was. "Sounds like a houseful."

"It was all right for a little while. My stepmother liked the fact my father had some pull in our community. She thought he could achieve more, though, so she pushed him to go after things he wouldn't have before. Soon, he was spending a lot of time at the Light Castle and interacting with a ton of influential people. My stepmother saw that as a way to get her daughters married to some rich Fae. And it worked."

While the story sounded fine, Sorcha had a feeling it would not end well. She didn't say anything, simply laid her hand against his chest, and waited for him to continue.

"Things were going along great. Until they weren't. My father got himself into a scheme that backfired on him, and it sent our family into ruin. My father was out of his league. He had no idea what to do. But my stepmother did."

A shiver of apprehension ran through Sorcha. She'd never met the woman, but she didn't like Cathal's stepmother at all.

He paused for a moment, then said, "She came to me and told me it was my responsibility to see that the wrong done to our family was put to rights since my father couldn't. I had left the house many years before since she and I were clashing already then. She wanted me to become like my father, and I had no interest in politics. I knew the only way I'd find happiness was to leave. So, I did, and I joined the Queen's Guard. However, when I left, there was no one to tell my father that my stepmother's ideas weren't always good. So, when she told me what had happened to him, I was outraged. The biggest mistake I made was believing everything she told me."

CHAPTER FIFTEEN

Cathal felt the same rage that used to control him begin to return. Then, Sorcha's hand began to rub softly across his chest. It helped him combat the storm of anger and return to the story.

"She told me my father had been tricked by two of his friends into investing their entire fortune into some business. The friends had known it was doomed to fail, and they laughed as he not only lost his money but also became a laughingstock amid those at court. I've always hated court because it's just a cruel place."

Sorcha smiled softly, nodding.

"I got the names of the men and immediately went after them. I spent hours torturing the first one, trying to get the truth out of him.

He kept telling me that he had no idea what I was talking about, that he was the one who had lost his investment. But I didn't believe him. I kept thinking about how I'd let my father down by leaving. Guilt rode me hard, and I lost myself to the anger. I killed the Light. But I didn't stop there. I went to the second so-called friend of my father's and began the torture anew with him. He said the same as the first. That he was the one who had lost his fortune. I didn't mean to kill him, but I did. And as I stood staring down at his body, it occurred to me that I hadn't thought to see my father first and get details from him."

Sorcha touched his face, sorrow in her eyes. "Did you go see him then?"

"I did," Cathal told her. "I was so wrapped up in finding the truth that I didn't stop to think about what I'd done—or the changes in my appearance. The minute my father saw me, he was appalled. When I tried to tell him why I'd done what I did, he wouldn't listen. That's when I saw my stepmother standing to the side with a smile on her face. I left the house that night, thinking I'd never see my father again. I was so distraught over what I'd done, believing it had been to save my sire, that I couldn't stand to be around anyone. I couldn't return to the Queen's Guard as a Dark, nor did I want to go to the Dark Palace. I didn't know what to do, so I went into the forest alone to try and sort myself out."

"Did you?" Sorcha asked.

He tugged at the auburn ringlet around his finger. "I wish I had before the note from my father reached me. It said that he wanted to talk, that he'd discovered what his wife had done to me, and he wanted to apologize. I didn't hesitate. I immediately went to the location. Except it wasn't my father there, it was my stepmother with the family of the men I'd slain."

Sorcha leaned her head forward. "What happened next?"

"They killed me."

"I'm sorry. They did what?" she asked, blinking as if she weren't sure she'd heard him correctly.

Cathal shot her a rueful smile. "They killed me."

"But…how are you here if they…you, know, killed you?"

"Magic."

Sorcha lowered her gaze to the bed. Then she asked, "Why did your stepmother want you out of the picture? Why did she lie to you?"

"Apparently, my father discovered that she'd been having an affair. In fact, she'd strayed twice—with the men I'd killed. She wanted them out of the way so my father couldn't confront them. To add insult to injury, she talked my father into the investment as well as into dragging the two men with him. After they'd sunk all their money into the business, my stepmother convinced my father not to do it."

"In other words, she helped to ruin those other men and used your father, as well."

Cathal nodded. "Exactly. She had gotten used to the money and prestige, but my father got tired of it. He wanted a quiet life, but she didn't. He became suspicious of her. She did whatever she could to keep things going how she wanted. When it all began to fall apart, she devised another plan. One that would turn my father against me."

"And turn you Dark."

"She knew exactly what to say. My father was everything to me. We were very close. I never begrudged him the happiness he'd found with his second wife, but I wasn't happy there. He accepted that. Yet, after I left, we drifted apart. He had other children to take care of and see to."

Sorcha licked her lips. "You blamed yourself for what happened."

"I did for a long time. You see, I was old enough to remember the Fae Realm before it was destroyed. I remember how happy we were there as a family. When we came to Earth, we found a new life. One that included my stepmother."

"I'm so sorry," Sorcha said as she leaned forward and kissed him. "What you did, you did for the love of your family. You might have taken it too far, but you're not to blame for all of it. Your stepmother instigated it all."

He smiled at her, falling harder by the second. "You don't need to say any of that. I know exactly what I did. I killed two men, and it doesn't matter the reasons why. I should've gone to my father first. Had I, none of that would've happened."

"But you wouldn't be whatever it is you are now. You wouldn't have helped me in the storm when I twisted my ankle, and you wouldn't have been at the Fairy Pools to stop that Light. I don't care what your coloring is. It's what's in your heart that counts," she told him.

Cathal pulled her against him, holding her close. He never wanted the night to end, but there was no stopping the coming dawn. "You told me your story. I wanted you to know mine."

"Thank you," she whispered.

He blew out a breath. "I want you to know that I won't let any of those other Fae harm you. Ever."

"You plan on watching over me always?" she asked with a smile as she looked up at him.

Cathal knew in that instant that the answer was a resounding yes. He parted his lips to tell her just that when someone cleared their throat from the living room.

"Just wanted you two to know I'm here," Aisling said.

Sorcha giggled and placed another quick kiss on his lips. "Guess that means we need to get up."

He wanted to drag her back and tell her to ignore Aisling, but he wouldn't. They had plans to make and an attack to get ready for. As much as he knew Sorcha's idea was dangerous, it was also the right one. Something was definitely off. And if Aisling was back, then she must have news.

Cathal forced himself to release Sorcha. Before her feet hit the floor, he used magic to put their clothes back on. She grinned at him and shot him a wink. He watched her walk from the room as he stayed behind. He didn't try to stand because he knew his knees wouldn't hold him.

Not when he realized that he loved her.

"Cathal?" Aisling called.

He cleared his throat twice before he could answer. "Coming."

When he walked into the living room, the two females were

sitting on the sofa. He chose the chair Sorcha had used earlier, thinking distance from her might be just what he needed to clear his head.

Aisling looked between them. "I've been trying to untangle lie after lie after lie."

"What did you find?" Sorcha asked.

Aisling flattened her lips as she speared a look at Cathal. "You were right, Sorcha. There is more than this thing about the ritual. It actually goes back to your father."

Cathal frowned at the news. His gaze jerked to Sorcha to find her doing her best to digest this latest tidbit. "What about her sire?" he asked.

"That's the thing, I'm not exactly sure." Aisling blew out a frustrated breath. "It didn't take long to hear that a Fae had taken out a contract, looking for his half-mortal daughter. I found that too coincidental, so I paid a visit to a few people. Turns out, no one knows if the Fae is Light or Dark. All they know is that the reward is huge."

Cathal's anger began to grow. "And this nonsense about getting Sorcha pregnant?"

"I'm guessing that's what some Fae think to do, to ensure they not only get the reward but also get into the family. The word is that it's a very prominent family." Aisling shrugged and looked at Sorcha. "I wish I could say it was just a rumor, but it's all anyone is talking about throughout the Fae."

Sorcha sat back and looked at Cathal. "Well, now we know why the Fae have suddenly decided to show up. And why they're so intent on getting me to go with them."

"They lay one hand on you, it'll be the last thing they do." He didn't care that fury laced his voice or that the threat might push Sorcha away from him. He'd promised to watch over her, and he was going to do just that.

Aisling looked between them. "Look, big guy, I hear you, but we need to be careful. We have rules we need to follow."

"She's right," Sorcha said. "Aisling found out a few things. Now, it's my turn to get to the truth."

Cathal barely heard either of them. He knew he had to answer to Death, but there was no way he would let anyone or anything harm Sorcha. She was…everything…to him. He nodded.

"What are you talking about?" Aisling asked.

Sorcha sat up and smiled. "Cathal and I talked."

"Oh, is that what you were doing?" Aisling interrupted with a roll of her eyes.

Cathal watched as a blush stained Sorcha's cheeks, and her emerald eyes met his. His heart swelled, love filling every particle of his being. He couldn't believe his path had crossed with hers. But now that he'd met her, he wasn't sure he could ever let her go.

The thing was, he might not have to if she agreed. Death now allowed the Reapers who found love to have their women and still continue to do her bidding. But the question was whether Sorcha would leave her human world behind for one on another realm with the Reapers. He was pretty sure he knew the answer.

"We did talk," Sorcha told Aisling with a saucy look. Then she ruined it with a bright smile. "As well as other things."

Aisling shot a look of surprise at Cathal. "Well, well. Sorry I interrupted, but I figured this was important."

"It is," Cathal told her.

Sorcha nodded. "I'm going to confront a Fae out there. I asked Cathal if both of you could be close when I do, but hiding so none of the other Fae can see you. Just in case I get into trouble and need help."

Once more, Aisling's red eyes landed on him. Cathal didn't acknowledge the question in her gaze.

"Of course, we will," Aisling said. "But…you can do magic. You're a Halfling. The bit of Fae magic within your veins will make your Druid magic stronger. If what we saw with Usaeil is any indication, you're incredibly powerful, Sorcha. I'm not sure you even need us."

And there it was. The very thing that had been in the back of Cathal's mind. Sorcha had asked him for help, had put her life in his hands when no one else ever had. But the simple fact was that she didn't need him. Or anyone.

"Cathal?" Aisling prodded.

He nodded woodenly to Sorcha. "Aisling is right. You are powerful."

"So powerful that I wasn't able to save my family," Sorcha said, though there was no heat in her words. She looked at the floor for several moments before she lifted her head and looked into his eyes. "I'd rather have you near, regardless if I do magic or not."

"Then I'll be there."

Aisling glanced at him. "*We'll* be there."

CHAPTER SIXTEEN

What in the world had she been thinking? Sorcha had actually believed that she could stand before a Fae and demand they tell her what she wanted to know. She must have gone daft for a few moments because now that she stood outside, she wanted nothing more than to turn around and run back into the house.

But she didn't. No matter how terrified she was of not only facing the Fae coming for her but also how she would respond if they told her the truth, she would never forgive herself if she didn't at least attempt to get some answers.

She didn't turn around and look at the house as she walked the property. Cathal and Aisling hadn't followed her out. They'd told her they would leave the house in a way that ensured that no one would see them but said they would keep an eye on her and be there if she got into trouble. Sorcha wanted to laugh at that because she didn't see how she could come face-to-face with the other Fae and *not* get into trouble.

As she walked, her thoughts went back to her trip to Ireland. The Skye Druids had been so upset about the prospect of other Druids forming a group to follow the Others that it was all Sorcha had thought about, as well. It had never entered her mind that there could be something more in store for her. Something potentially bigger.

After all, the Others—as well as Usaeil—had left scars upon them that were still raw and festering. Not to mention, whatever these Fae wanted with Sorcha had nothing to do with the other Druids on the isle. So why should any of them have taken note? It wasn't as if Sorcha had actually been a part of the Druid community over the last ten years. She might be blood to some, but she had made it known that she wanted nothing to do with any of them. If they had seen the Fae, they hadn't been worried enough about them to check in with her.

And she couldn't be upset about that. She had gone out of her way to distance herself from them, telling them in no uncertain terms that she wanted nothing to do with the Druid way of life anymore.

Though she still wasn't sure why she had gone to Ireland. No, that wasn't true. She had gone because her cousin had asked for her help. Rhona was one of the few who kept in touch with Sorcha whether she wanted it or not. And not once in all those years had Rhona asked Sorcha for anything. How then, when she *had* come to her, could Sorcha say no?

Looking back, Sorcha was glad that she had gone to Ireland. She hadn't been happy at the time, but it had brought Cathal into her life. Just thinking of him made her smile. She knew he had secrets, and she was all right with that. Mainly because she accepted that he wouldn't remain in her life. Odd how her mum hadn't bothered to tell her about her father, and yet Sorcha had nearly followed in her mother's footsteps. Well, in all cases, she *had* followed her mother. She had fallen in love with a Fae. What Sorcha wouldn't do was get pregnant or believe that Cathal might want her as his.

She tried not to feel resentment or anger at that thought, but she couldn't quite manage it. For all she knew, one of Cathal's secrets was that he was married. She really hoped not. The one thing she could never forgive was a person cheating on their lover with another. She'd only had one boyfriend do that to her, and it had been the worst pain she'd ever experienced.

Sorcha stopped when she got to the fence. This was one of the places where Cathal had urged her to go. Apparently, a Fae had been here, standing for hours, simply staring at her house. There was no one here now, however.

She clicked her tongue and held up the carrot. One of the mares in the pasture jerked her head up. She didn't always come with treats, but that never stopped the animals from trotting over to her for some petting and soft words. She'd always loved horses. They were magnificent animals.

As the horse drew closer, it slowed to a walk, neighing softly. She smiled and held out the carrot as an offering. The animal extended its neck to take the vegetable instead of coming closer. That alerted Sorcha that something wasn't right.

"What's wrong, girl?" she asked the mare.

The horse chewed the carrot. Once it was gone, the animal took a tentative step to the fence. Sorcha held out her hand, waiting for the horse. As the mare paused, Sorcha suddenly had a feeling that she shouldn't have put her hand over the fence. She lowered her arm, her heart pounding. It could be nothing more than her imagination getting the better of her. And no one knew better than she just how active her thoughts could be.

Still, she couldn't help but feel as if she had just barely avoided being grabbed. Sorcha hoped it was nothing more than her imaginings, but she didn't think so. She wished she could take hold of Cathal's hand. It helped to know that he was near. It was too bad he wasn't right beside her, though.

Funny, she had always been so proud of the fact that she didn't need anyone for anything. She managed things on her own. Her mother had begun that when she taught both Sorcha and Molly that there was no reason the two of them couldn't do anything anyone else did. Her mother had gotten many tools over the years, and thanks to online videos now, Sorcha had learned to fix all sorts of problems in her house and with her car.

And she hadn't done any of it with magic.

Not that there weren't times when she wanted to do magic. Sometimes, she woke with it running through her so potently that all she had to do was think of what she wanted to do, and it likely would've happened. But she hadn't let herself.

If she hadn't relied on magic that day with her mum and Molly, then they might still be alive. She'd been overconfident and arrogant, and she'd paid a heavy price for it. Sorcha wasn't going to allow that to happen again. Magic was nice to have. It was handy in some instances, but it couldn't be counted on to save lives.

She was so lost in thought that when the mare jerked her head up, it startled Sorcha. She started to turn away when something caught her attention out of the corner of her eye. Sorcha did a double take, her gaze immediately landing on a man standing a few meters away. He was beautiful with short black hair and bright silver eyes, and he was attired immaculately. That revealed a Fae more than most anything. The fact that they were so vain they had to dress so perfectly showed their true colors.

Except for Cathal. He was the exception to the rule.

Well, if she were honest, that also extended to Aisling. She was very different from the other Fae Sorcha had encountered.

"Hello," he said, smiling.

She had already pegged him as a Fae, so his Irish accent didn't surprise her. Sorcha gave him a nod. "I believe you're trespassing on my neighbor's property."

"Am I?" he asked, not seeming to care.

"You are. He doesn't take kindly to such transgressions. You should leave now before you're seen."

The Fae smiled, showing even, white teeth. "Perhaps you'd like to invite me onto your property."

"Why would I do that?"

Without missing a beat, he said, "So we can chat."

Sorcha wanted to tell him to kiss off, but she was out here for a reason. She needed information. However, that didn't mean she would do something stupid like invite a Fae onto her property.

Unless it's Cathal.

She almost smiled at the thought of the Dark. Sorcha inwardly gave herself a shake so she could focus and stay on task. She looked the Fae up and down. Because they lived so long, it was hard to determine their exact age. "Why would a Fae want to chat with me?"

"Ah." One side of his mouth lifted in a smile. "I wondered if you knew what I was."

"I'm a Skye Druid. Of course, I know who the Fae are."

He bowed his head, giving her that. "I hear you don't ever leave your estate."

She almost laughed at the fact that he'd called her little plot of land and the cottage an *estate*, but she managed to hold it in. "I like my privacy. However, I've seen a lot more Fae around than usual. You wouldn't happen to know why that is, would you?"

"I would."

Sorcha ignored the fact that his smile grew as if he had caught her. "Care to share?"

"Care to invite me onto your land?" he countered.

She gave a shake of her head and turned on her heel. As she walked away, she said, "No, I wouldn't."

Three steps later, he called out. "Wait. Please."

Sorcha stopped, knowing that now was her chance to return to the cottage and forget this wild idea of hers. She scanned the area, wishing she knew exactly where Cathal was. He was there somewhere, and that was enough to give her the courage she needed to continue. She drew in a deep breath and faced the Light Fae.

"I'm sorry," he said as he held up his hands and walked closer to the fence.

He ignored the mare, who hurriedly walked away. Sorcha

wasn't sure, but she didn't think that animals usually shied away from the Fae. What was it about this one that caused the horse to give him a wide berth? Whatever it was, Sorcha wasn't going to take it lightly.

Sorcha crossed her arms over her chest. "Why is it so important for you to come onto my property? And if I hear another lie that it's to impregnate me with your seed so you'll never have to be forced from this planet, I'm walking away now."

The Fae smiled. "You're as smart as I thought you'd be."

That got her interest, but she didn't let it show. "Why is that?"

"Do you know you're a Halfling? A mortal with Fae blood in your veins?"

She shrugged. "I might have heard something about that. What does it matter? I'm a Skye Druid. That means more to me than being a Halfling."

"You wouldn't say that if you had been raised with the Fae."

Sorcha narrowed her eyes on the Light. His words were as smooth as silk, but she didn't buy any of it. "How about you just tell me what it is you want me to know. You can say it there just as easily as you can say it on my side of the fence. And just so we're clear, I'm not inviting you onto my land."

"I'm really sorry to hear that," he said as he frowned. "I'd be happy to tell you what you want to know, but I'll only do it if I'm standing next to you on your side of the property line."

"I figured you'd say something like that," she retorted.

His black brows rose in his too-perfect face. "No counter?"

"I told you my offer. You don't want to tell me, that's fine. I'm not going to let a Fae onto my property."

"Oh, now that isn't entirely true, is it?"

She blinked, wondering if he knew about Cathal and Aisling. "Shall I repeat my sentence?"

"There was a Fae here before."

Sorcha shot him a bored expression. "I'm sure there have been Fae on all of Skye before. That doesn't mean I'm going to allow one onto my land now. You want something from me, and I'm not going to give it to you until I know the truth. I'm fine not hearing what you have to say. Are you fine not getting whatever it is you want from me?"

"You're just like your mother."

The words were like a knife cutting straight into Sorcha's heart. Her arms dropped limply to her sides. She knew without asking who this man was. This was her chance to ask him why he hadn't come for her mother, why he had broken her mum's heart. But, more importantly, she wanted to know what he was doing here now.

"I see I've caught you by surprise." His lips twisted ruefully as he put his hands on the fence. "I've been standing here for hours, thinking of how to tell you who I am. I'm sorry it didn't come out better."

Sorcha decided to play stupid. "Who are you? I'm shocked because you act as if you knew my mother."

Her words caught him by surprise. He stilled. "I told you that you're a Halfling, and that you act like your mother."

"A lot of people tell me that. If you think that will make me think you've slept with my mum, you're wrong." The words were difficult to get out, but she was glad she'd said them.

He swallowed and shook his head as he looked down. "She never told you about me?"

"No." That's all she was going to give him.

The Fae blew out a breath and raised his gaze to hers, no longer seeming quite so confident. "My name is Eamon. I met your mother twenty-nine years ago tomorrow. As soon as I saw her, she claimed my heart."

"Why should I believe you?"

"I thought she would've told you about me. Where is she? Bring her out here, and she'll tell you the truth."

Sorcha's throat clogged with emotion as she said, "Mum died ten years ago."

The shock on Eamon's face was real. "I didn't know."

"If you're my father, then why are you here now?"

"I've been…away. I couldn't get back here."

Sorcha rolled her eyes. "Convenient."

"It also happens to be the truth."

She quirked a brow, waiting for him to tell her more.

He blew out a frustrated breath. "I wasn't supposed to touch your mother. I wasn't supposed to fall in love either, but I did. I went against my queen, and for that, Usaeil locked me in a prison so I couldn't return."

"Usaeil is dead. You could be making that up."

"She put me in a cell she designed, not the Light Prison. When she died, the magic holding me evaporated. That's when I began looking for your mother. I saw you and realized who you were."

Sorcha wanted to believe him. If this were true, it would mean that her father wasn't a bad person. But she couldn't forget the way the mare had moved away from him. "Tell me why the other Fae are here for me?"

"They're looking for me."

She gave a snort of laughter. "You were doing so good, then you had to go and ruin it. You aren't my father."

Sorcha spun around and started back to the house. There was a sound of something behind her, then she heard Cathal shout her name. She looked over her shoulder to see an iridescent ball coming straight at her. It was pure instinct that had her diving to the side.

CHAPTER SEVENTEEN

He was going to kill the Fae. The moment Cathal saw the ball of magic being thrown at Sorcha, he started toward the Light. But Aisling held him back.

"Get yourself together," she whispered through clenched teeth.

He glanced down at her, surprised by her strength. Then his gaze jerked to Sorcha. She was on the ground, the magic having missed her by a foot. The Fae sneered at her. Cathal fisted his hands.

"Get ahold of yourself," Aisling ground out.

They were close enough to both Sorcha and the Fae to be heard, which was why Aisling whispered. Fortunately, Sorcha and the Fae were too focused on each other to take notice.

Sorcha jumped to her feet and glared at the Fae. "Take a good look, wanker, because this is as close as you'll ever get to me."

He laughed. "You think you're smarter than me? Think again. It doesn't matter if you're a Halfling or a Skye Druid, you'll never have what it takes to best me."

"I just did."

"You think you can keep us off your land forever?" The Fae threw back his head and laughed.

It sent a chill down Cathal's spine. He glanced at Aisling to see her staring intently at the Fae.

Sorcha suddenly smiled. Then she yelled, "Hey, Fae! Any Fae in the area? Show yourselves."

To Cathal's shock, twenty other Fae appeared. Both Dark and Light, male and female. But not one of them was on Sorcha's property.

She let her gaze scan over them, completely ignoring the one who had attempted to harm her. "I hear there is interest in coming onto my land. I also hear it's because one of you wants to get me pregnant."

One of the female Dark barked with laughter. "I don't want to get you pregnant."

Sorcha walked closer to the Dark on the opposite side of the property and that fence. Cathal stayed near her while Aisling remained behind.

"Of course, you don't," Sorcha told the Dark. "What is it you *do* want from me?"

The female shrugged, her pixie-cut black and silver hair barely moving in the wind. "You really think you'll get one of us to tell you something other than a lie?"

"Good point," Sorcha said with a twist of her lips. "If that's the case, then there's no reason for any of you to be here because I'm never letting you onto my property."

An older Light Fae male spoke up then. "You won't have a choice soon."

Sorcha's gaze swung to him. "And why's that?"

"Because you've been protected. That's ending."

Cathal frowned, his mind racing while trying to figure out what was going on.

Sorcha nodded slowly. "That's a plausible story."

"It isn't a story." Silver eyes held Sorcha's as the Fae blew out a breath. "There's a bounty on your head. There has been since the moment you were born."

Cathal found his gaze locked on Sorcha. He knew that he should be looking at the others, but he was too concerned about her. He couldn't tell if anything she was being told affected her. She had already been through so much. He didn't want her to suffer any more pain.

Sorcha licked her lips. "One Fae told me he was my father."

"Your father is the one who has been protecting you," the Light told her.

Cathal moved closer to Sorcha so he stood just a few feet behind her. It allowed him to watch her as well as the Light she spoke with. The other Fae gave the Fae dirty looks, which made Cathal think that he might be telling Sorcha the truth.

The Light didn't seem to notice or care that the others were coming closer to him. His gaze was on Sorcha alone. "Your father's name is Eamon, and he wanted nothing more than to come here and meet you himself. He's wanted it for so very long."

Cathal knew how words regarding a parent could confuse a person. He'd let someone do that to him once. The problem was, he wasn't sure if this Fae spoke lies, or if it was the truth. He turned his head to Aisling to find her staring at him. She gave him a nod to let him know that she was listening, as well.

"Is this where you tell me I act just like my mother?" Sorcha retorted.

The Fae smiled sadly. "I never met your mother. I wish I had come to see her, but I...well, I listened to others instead and didn't."

No sooner had the words left his mouth than a ball of magic slammed into him from behind. The Light fell to his knees, pain contorting his features. Sorcha started to go to him but decided against it at the last minute.

"Stay here," Cathal told her. "Aisling is going to help him."

He'd never told Sorcha that he could be veiled indefinitely. She didn't seem surprised to hear him so close beside her. Nor did she look for him. Most people would've demanded that he tell them what was going on. But not his Sorcha.

He watched as Aisling took out the female Light who had attacked the male. Unfortunately, the original attack on the Light seemed to broadcast to all the others that it was time to kill the Fae.

Cathal needed to help Aisling, but he didn't want to leave Sorcha there alone. One stray orb of magic could find its way to her. He debated things for a second before he told her, "Get to the house and stay low."

Without a word, Sorcha pivoted and ran to the house. Cathal noted that the first Fae she'd spoken with near the fence watched it all with interest. He was the only one who wasn't attacking the Light who had spoken with Sorcha.

Cathal didn't think about it any longer as he joined Aisling, and the two of them—while still veiled—quickly dispatched those closest to the Light. The others soon got the hint and left. The last was the Fae near the fence. He stared in Cathal's direction, but it didn't matter. No one other than Death or another Reaper could see through the veil they used.

The coughing of the Light near his feet drew Cathal's attention. He looked down to see the older Fae on his hands and knees as he spat blood. He had several wounds, some severe, but there was no reason to think that he wouldn't heal. At least he would now that the others were no longer attacking him.

The Light lifted his head and looked around to see that he was alone. He wiped the blood from his mouth and moved to a nearby tree where he sat against it and blew out a breath. His shoulders sagged as regret and grief filled his face.

Aisling lifted a brow, asking if they should show themselves to the Light. Cathal shook his head. He motioned for her to wait as he teleported into Sorcha's cabin. The moment he did, he lowered his veil so she could see him.

She was huddled in the kitchen near some cabinets. At the sight of Cathal, she gave him a smile. "Is it over?"

"For now," he said and held out his hand.

She took it so he could pull her to her feet. "What about the Fae who was talking to me?"

"The one who was attacked is still out there. I think he wants to finish what he began."

"I don't know if I can believe him."

Cathal tugged at a ringlet, remembering how close she had come to being hurt by one of the orbs of magic. "Someone is going to a lot of trouble to make sure you don't find out something. The shite about getting you with child is just that. The more I'm hearing, the more I'm inclined to believe that there *is* a price on your head."

"But why? I didn't even know I was a Halfling until you told me yesterday."

He shrugged and dropped his arm. "We won't find that out until you finish talking to the Light."

"Will you be with me?"

"Aye."

She gave a nod. "Then I'll do it."

He frowned then because he'd been fully prepared for her to ask him how he had been so close but not visible. "Aren't you going to ask me how?"

"It's one of your secrets," she told him simply.

"Don't you want to know?"

She laughed softly. "Of course, I do. But I also respect the fact that you might not be able to tell me. If you wanted me to know, then you'd say."

The problem was, he did want her to know. The other problem was that he was now up against one of the most significant rules the Reapers had. No Fae could know about them. Somehow, the other Reapers had gotten by that regarding their mates. But Cathal wasn't sure he would be able to do the same.

Before he knew it, words fell from his lips. "Fae can veil themselves. It means we can hide from others."

"You become invisible."

He issued a single nod. "Most can only do it for a few seconds. I'm…different."

"That's what you did out there? You veiled yourself so you could stay near me?" she asked.

"Aye."

"That's amazing." She smiled. "And a little scary. Are you telling me there could be Fae around now, and we wouldn't know?"

"No," he told her. "It takes a lot of power to hold a veil for even ten seconds. You'd know if someone was there."

"But you can hold yours for…?"

He swallowed, unsure if he'd made the right choice in telling her. Then he figured if he was in for a penny, he was in for a pound. "As long as I want."

"Wow. You must be extremely powerful."

Cathal didn't say anything to that. He cleared his throat. "I think you'd better get back out there and see if you can learn any more."

"All right." She walked to the door and looked over her shoulder at him. The smile she flashed him made him giddy.

The moment she walked out the door, he veiled himself and teleported right beside her.

CHAPTER EIGHTEEN

Sorcha was still reeling from what Cathal had shared with her. She hadn't had any idea that a Fae could remain veiled for as long as they wanted. At least she knew Cathal was near her, and that was enough for her.

She spotted the Fae near a tree and walked to him. Sorcha had learned her lesson the first time and didn't get close to the fence. Neither said anything as they stared at each other.

The Light planted one foot on the ground and rested his arm over his knee. "I didn't think you'd come back out."

"I didn't either. Now that I have, perhaps you can continue what you were saying."

"I'm not sure it's going to do any good." He looked at the sky for a heartbeat. "Eamon always talked about Skye. It was one place I'd never gone. I hadn't intended to ever come here after what happened to him. And yet, here I am."

Sorcha eyed the wounds over his body. "You obviously felt it was something you had to do. Otherwise, you wouldn't have taken such a beating."

"I want you to know that your father would be here if he could. Not being able to see you has destroyed him."

"He's Fae. I'm sure he'll get over it," Sorcha said with a shrug. She didn't want this male or anyone else to know that she wanted nothing more than to meet her father.

The Light chuckled softly. "You sound just like him. He was proud and stubborn, but he was a good Fae, a good brother."

Sorcha blinked, understanding taking hold that she was talking to her uncle. "What is your name?"

"Eddie."

Then something else hit her. "You keep saying *was*."

"Your father was attacked a few nights ago. It weakened him enough that the shield preventing other Fae from knowing you're a Halfling was lowered. It allowed the others to locate you."

Her mind worked quickly to find a solution. Then she realized there already was one. "Eamon is a Fae. He'll heal, just as you will."

"I wish that were true," her uncle said. "He's dying. He's the only thing preventing others from gaining access to this property. The second the last breath leaves his body, they'll swarm you."

"Why?" she asked, not understanding.

He shook his head, regret filling his silver eyes. "Your father had a wife when he met your mother. It wasn't a good marriage, and they had gone their separate ways for some time. When your father returned to Ireland to get a divorce, his wife wanted to know why. She liked the arrangement they had. She got to use the family name as well as our money while doing whatever she liked with whomever she liked. Your father wanted to change things, and she wasn't going to allow that."

Sorcha wished she had something to hold onto to help her stay standing. "He promised my mother he'd return."

"He was going to. I was with him, trying to talk him into changing his mind. I couldn't understand what it was about the mortal that drew him. In one last bid to hold onto what she had, his wife sent men after your mother. Eamon and I were able to stop them, but he realized that his wife would never stop. Even if he got the divorce, she'd keep coming after your mother. We stood right here under this tree that last night as he tried to find a way to have the woman he loved."

A tear slipped down Sorcha's cheek.

"To stop his wife, Eamon went back to Delma and their sham of a marriage. What he didn't know was that she had Fae watching your mother to make sure he never returned. One of those spies learned that your mother was pregnant with you. Eamon's wife sent mercenaries to kill both you and your mother. My brother stopped her again, and that began the war between our families. From that moment until now, your father has protected you. His wife's hatred moved from your mother to you, so he believed that all he had to do was keep you safe."

Sorcha shook her head as more tears came. "Don't say it. Please, don't say it."

"Your father's wife was the one who ensured your mother died. Delma set everything in place, then misdirected your magic. Your sister was a casualty of their war, I'm afraid."

Sorcha fell to her knees as she doubled over from the pain of her uncle's words. She didn't want to hear anymore. It was too painful.

Her uncle continued. "I've never seen your father so furious. He went after his wife in an epic battle that killed many in our families. He ended up wounding her gravely, enough that she went into hiding and left you alone. At least, that's what he thought. He let his guard down little by little, and that's when she struck again. I haven't spoken to him in ten years, not since his anger tore our family apart. I thought his ploy of being wounded was just that, something to get me to see him. But one look and I knew he had little time left. That's when he told me one of his friends betrayed him and led him into a trap that his wife had devised. She told him she'd put a price on your head. It's big enough to draw any and all Fae to you."

Rage the likes of which Sorcha had never experienced before filled her. It pushed away the grief and the pain and dried her tears. She lifted her head to her uncle. The knowledge that she hadn't been the one to cause her mother's and sister's deaths was like someone had lit a match. And she was the powder keg.

"I know that look," her uncle said. "It was in your father's eyes the day he tried to kill his wife for your mother's murder. You're the only thing that has kept him going these past years. I'm here on his behalf to tell you all of this. But also to ensure that you have a fighting chance against those coming for you."

Sorcha fisted her hands as resentment and fury churned to mix with the magic that thrummed through her. There was no stopping it even if she wanted to. She had imprisoned herself for something that hadn't been her fault. Her mother had lived alone for nearly thirty years, pining for a man she didn't think loved her. All because another woman couldn't accept that her marriage and the life she craved was over.

Her uncle laughed, though the sound held no humor. "You're a strong Druid, and you're a powerful Halfling. But neither of those will help you now. You might be able to live for a little while, but you'll constantly be on the run."

"Not if I kill her," Sorcha said. "Where can I find her?"

He blew out a breath and laboriously climbed to his feet. "Our two families united in marriage because both had political sway. The difference was that her family lost most of their money. She's shrewd and cunning."

"And very full of herself. I'm going to do the one thing she'll never think of. I'm going to go after her," Sorcha declared.

Her uncle stared at her for a full minute without speaking. Then he bowed his head to her. "Before you do that, let me take you to see your father. There's still time."

It was on the tip of Sorcha's tongue to agree, but she wasn't going anywhere without Cathal. "Tell me where he is. I'll get there on my own."

"There isn't time for you to drive," her uncle said with a frown.

Sorcha lifted her chin as she got to her feet. "I never said I was driving."

A slow smile pulled at her uncle's mouth.

CHAPTER NINETEEN

"This is fekking nonsense," Cathal said after the Light had vanished, and he dropped his veil to face Sorcha.

She, however, didn't seem to care what his thoughts were. "I'm going. I'd like for you to take me."

"You haven't used magic in ten years. Now, you want to charge in after a woman who is hell-bent on ending your life?" he bellowed. "For the love of all that's magical, someone help me out here! Aisling?"

The Dark dropped her veil as she walked toward them. "Don't look to me to agree with you. I'm on Sorcha's side."

"For fek's sake," he mumbled and dropped his chin to his chest.

After a moment, he blew out a frustrated breath and looked up to see Sorcha and Aisling standing together. "This is suicide, Sorcha."

Aisling lifted a shoulder. "Not if we're with her."

"That wasn't our mission," he reminded her.

The Dark glared at him, anger shooting from her gaze. "Did you hear nothing of what her uncle said? How can you stand there and act as if it doesn't matter?"

"You think it didn't affect me?" he asked, fury filling his voice and expression. "I want to find this bitch myself and rip her limb from limb, but I'd like to keep Sorcha alive more."

Aisling propped her hands on her hips. "We were sent here to find out about Sorcha. Well, we have. But there's more to learn. If she's going after the crazy stepmum, then I'm going with her to do what I can."

"That's walking a line we might cross."

Sorcha walked to him and put a hand on his chest. "Then don't come. I don't want you to do anything that goes against what you believe."

"It isn't that." Though he wasn't sure he wanted to tell her the truth. It was a long story, and right now, they didn't have time for any of that.

"Thank you for everything," Sorcha said and rose up on her toes to place a kiss on his cheek. Then she faced Aisling. "Can you take me to my father?"

Before Cathal could ask Sorcha to wait, Aisling took hold of her and teleported. Cathal ground his teeth together and followed the duo to the address in Ireland that the uncle had given Sorcha. However, he made sure to appear veiled and behind them. Aisling likely knew he'd follow, so she didn't look for him. Sorcha was too taken by the act of arriving at her father's home to even think of looking around her.

Cathal watched as the two of them walked over the estate grounds to the manor house. Fae stood guard everywhere. To his trained eye, Cathal knew they were experienced men who knew how to do their job. Cathal wanted to go into the manor with Sorcha, but he decided to stay outside and make a few rounds himself.

If Eamon was as close to death as his brother had said, then Sorcha didn't have long. And with as calculating as Eamon's wife was, Cathal didn't put anything past her.

It took a moment for Sorcha to realize why none of the guards along the estate had stopped her and Aisling. When she looked at the Dark and noticed that Aisling still had a hold of her, she then understood that she was veiled, just as Aisling was. As if sensing that she was about to speak, Aisling looked her way and put her finger to her lips.

Sorcha had heard her uncle speak of the wealth of the family, but she hadn't comprehended just what that might mean to a Fae. As she eyed the immaculate gardens, the perfectly trimmed hedges, and the beautiful and imposing stone manor that sat on what had to be at least fifty acres of land, she began to understand.

When they reached the gravel drive, Aisling dropped her hand and came to a stop. Sorcha halted beside her. Within seconds, shouts rose up from the guards, who then teleported to circle around them.

"Now is the time you talk," Aisling told her.

Sorcha swallowed and opened her mouth. Just as she was about to speak, a voice from the doorway ordered the guards to let them through. When the Fae moved back, Sorcha spotted her uncle. He motioned her forward hurriedly.

She ran to the door with Aisling at her heels. Sorcha didn't take the time to look at anything as her uncle teleported her and Aisling from the ground floor to a room somewhere in the manor. Then her gaze landed on the large four-poster bed and the man who lay there, propped up by several pillows.

He smiled, his silver eyes filled with happiness. "I never thought I'd be able to see you."

His voice was rough with pain, but it didn't diminish his obvious joy. She walked to the bed and looked down at the man who was her father. His black hair was kept on the long side. He wore navy silk pajamas that seemed to make his silver eyes even brighter. She couldn't see a wound, but she heard his labored breathing.

"Hello, Sorcha. I'm Eamon, your father. I wish I could've been there for you through the years. I wish you, your mum, and Molly could've lived here with me. It's what I wanted more than anything."

Tears filled her eyes, and she hastily blinked them back. Then she covered the hand on top of the blanket with hers. He turned his palm up and linked their fingers. There was still strength there.

Sorcha smiled and nodded. "That would've been nice. You were the love of Mum's life. I didn't find out about you until yesterday."

"You're here now. It's something I've always dreamed of." Then his smile died. "I'm sorry I didn't protect your mum better."

She shook her head and squeezed his hand. "That wasn't your fault. None of this is your fault."

"You have the kindness of your mother. It's what drew me to her. She was an amazing woman who deserved so much more."

"She gave Molly and me a good life."

He smiled, but his face creased with pain. It took him a moment before he could speak again. "I've left everything to you. Eddie knows this," he said, indicating his brother.

"I'd rather have you," Sorcha said.

"Ah, my darling. If I could give you that, I would. But if I can't give you that, the least I can do is make sure that you don't get involved in this war of mine. Delma will never be satisfied no matter how many people she has killed or makes suffer. Upon my death, a decree will go out, announcing you as my heir and under the protection of our family."

Sorcha frowned. "I don't understand how that's going to help. Weren't you under the protection of your family? She still got to you."

"Actually, I wasn't. When your mother was killed, I pulled my family into my war. The consequences were…severe. I wasn't banished from the family because I was the eldest son, but I wasn't included in it either. That ended the moment Delma had me attacked. The entirety of my family—which is considerable—will ensure that Delma, nor anyone else, will ever come after you."

"What of the price on her head?" Aisling asked.

Eamon glanced at the Dark before his gaze returned to Sorcha. "Should anyone ignore the protection that covers Sorcha, they will be hunted."

"I want to go after Delma for what she's done to you and my family," Sorcha said.

Her father shook his head. "She's not worth it. Live. That's what you can do to thwart her. By living, you give a gift to your mother and me. If you go after her, you'll give her exactly what she wants."

"You can't really expect me to do nothing about her," Sorcha said with a frown.

Eamon smiled softly. "Ignoring her will upset her more than going after her. Living as if you don't care about her will hurt much more than any type of magic used on her. I learned this too late. I'm telling you now so you don't make my same mistakes. I know you've not done magic in ten years. There will come a time when you'll want to use it. Don't use your magic to take a life. It'll twist you in ways you can't begin to comprehend. You'll know when it's time to use your power again."

Sorcha had to admit that his words made sense. "All right. I'll do as you've asked. It won't be easy, however."

"Nothing worthwhile ever is."

That made her think of Cathal. She wished he had come with her. Sorcha licked her lips and glanced at Aisling to see her standing by the door. "You didn't ask why I came with a Dark."

"What you do with your life is your business." He shrugged. "I know you're a good person. You couldn't have been raised by your mother and not be. If you are friendly with some Dark, then I trust that you know what you're doing."

Sorcha shrugged. "I'm not sure I do. I learned I was a Halfling shortly before I learned about you. Aisling and Cathal have helped to protect me. Without them, I wouldn't be standing here now."

"Then I owe them my thanks," he said as he smiled at Aisling.

Then he lowered his voice to Sorcha. "A Dark doesn't usually help unless they want something."

"They're different."

"Just be careful," he cautioned. "I might not have a right to tell you that because I wasn't there for you all these years, but as your father, I'm asking it of you."

Sorcha glanced out the large window to the rolling green hills. "When did you know you loved my mum?"

"The second I looked at her. Then she smiled at me." His face took on a faraway look filled with such love and happiness that it almost seemed wrong to watch him. Then he blinked and came back to himself. "Why do you ask?"

"Because I've fallen in love."

Her father's silver eyes were sharp and perceptive when he asked, "Cathal?"

She nodded, unable to hide her smile. "I wish you could meet him. He's amazing. He was once a Light, but he was betrayed by his stepmom and killed. He's—"

"He died?" her father asked.

Something in his tone made her hesitate. Then she looked at Aisling to find her shaking her head, her head lowered. Sorcha swung her gaze back at her father. "What?"

"You said Cathal was killed." Before her father could continue, he doubled over, his face contorted by agony.

Her uncle rushed to the bed to hold her father up. Sorcha stared helpless, unsure what to do or if she *could* do anything.

Aisling came up beside her. "You might want to think of leaving now."

"I'm not going anywhere," she snapped to the Dark.

Aisling simply looked at her. "I've seen this before. What he's going through is extremely painful."

"What is it?"

"Poison," her father rasped as he leaned back on the pillows and took in huge gulps of air. "Your friend is right. It is painful, and it's only going to get worse from here."

Sorcha looked him in the eye. "I don't care."

"I do," he replied with a tired smile. "I don't want your last memory of me to be one of me writhing in pain while the poison slowly works its way through my body. I got to meet you, to speak with you, and that is the best thing that could've happened to me."

She didn't want to cry anymore, but tears gathered anyway. "It's not fair that I just learned about you and met you, only to lose you."

"You won't lose me. I'll always be with you. Just as your mother is."

A tear fell down her face. "There's no way to fight the poison?"

"No, there isn't," Aisling said. "Trust me. I know."

Sorcha noted the look that passed between Aisling and Eamon, but she didn't comment on it. Not now, at least. She would ask Aisling about it later.

"Come," her father beckoned.

Sorcha walked to him and took the hand he offered. There was so much she wanted to say, but she didn't know where to even begin. So many questions rattled through her head, but she knew there wasn't time for any of them.

The breath he drew in was ragged. "I don't care how much Fae blood or Druid blood or mortal blood is in your veins. You're my daughter, and you're the only thing I'm going to miss when I go. At least I'll get to be with your mother once more. Now, I want you to go somewhere safe until this is over. Then my brother will find you."

She wanted to argue, but she didn't have the heart. Sorcha leaned in and wrapped her arms around her father. He was quick to return the embrace, holding her tightly for a brief moment. When she pulled away, there were tears in his eyes, as well. It wasn't fair that he was being taken from her. It made hate fill her heart, but she didn't want that either. She wanted only to feel the love they had shared briefly.

As she walked from the room with Aisling by her side, all she could think about was the years she hadn't cared if she had a father or not. Now, she knew that she had missed out on some truly amazing moments with a good man. None of it was fair. Not what had happened to keep him and her mother apart, not her mother's and sister's deaths, not her father's poisoning, and not the fact that she had finally found the other side of her family, only to lose her da that same day.

"It would be easy to give in to the anger," Aisling said as they walked down the last flight of stairs to the main floor.

Sorcha nodded. "I think I'm too filled with grief right now."

"It'll hit," the Dark warned. "Don't let it consume you. Nothing good comes from it."

She looked at the Fae. "You sound as if you speak from experience."

"Because I do," Aisling said.

Sorcha opened the door, and the two of them stepped over the threshold. As soon as they did, an orb of magic landed near Sorcha's feet.

CHAPTER TWENTY

Years of being a Queen's Guard as well as a Reaper had taught Cathal when to recognize the tension in the air that spelled impending battle. And he wasn't the only one. The Fae standing guard around the estate were on high alert.

The problem was, Cathal couldn't find anything that told him when or where the attack would happen. Yet his gut said it would. He kept his veil up and walked the property from one end to the other. Guards were strategically placed around the estate, but the majority of them were around the house.

Cathal looked at the manor, wondering where in the building Sorcha was. He didn't need to worry about the Halfling being protected there because Aisling would have that covered. With a sigh, he turned so the house was at his back. His gaze kept scanning the horizon. Something prickled the back of his mind, but he couldn't quite grasp what it was.

He was making another round of the perimeter of the manor when he glanced at one of the guards. Something about him didn't sit right with Cathal, though he couldn't put his finger on why. He got close to the guard and walked around the Fae, trying to figure out what it was that had caught his attention.

Then it hit him. He'd seen this Fae before—at Sorcha's cottage.

Cathal teleported into the manor. The sound of a door caught his attention. He spun around in time to see Sorcha and Aisling walking out. Time slowed to a crawl when the ball of magic crashed between the women. Without a thought for his own safety, Cathal jumped to them and grabbed hold of Sorcha to pull her back into the building.

He lowered his veil and examined her. "Are you hurt? Did any of it hit you?"

"I'm fine," she said, though her voice shook.

Cathal lifted his head to Aisling to see that her eyes were focused outside as she used the door for cover. "Who is it?"

"Anyone looking to take Sorcha's life," Aisling said. She then looked at Cathal. "Eamon is dying from poison. He's made it so Sorcha is listed as his heir. When he dies, she'll be safe."

Cathal glanced down at Sorcha, who had her arms wrapped around him. "Until then, she's fair game, I suppose."

"Unfortunately," Sorcha said with a shrug.

He wasn't going to stand there and wait for the bastards to find Sorcha. "I'm going out there."

"The hell you are," Sorcha said.

Cathal smiled as he looked down at her. "I'll be veiled. They'll never see me coming."

"Us," Aisling corrected. "Don't leave me out of some ass-kicking."

He nodded to her before returning his gaze to Sorcha. "Remain here. They'll never get to the house."

"I don't like this," Sorcha said.

Cathal pulled her against him and kissed her. "This is what Aisling and I do. You don't need to worry about us."

"That's right," Aisling said as she cracked her knuckles. "Come on, big guy. You can kiss her later. It's time for battle."

Cathal took one last look at Sorcha and pulled back from her arms before he and Aisling veiled themselves and rushed out the door. They made quick work of the men attacking the estate. If the guards realized what was going on, they gave no indication of it.

He kept looking for the guard who had been at Sorcha's. Because if there was one of them in disguise, there would be others. Cathal found him easily enough and quickly dispatched him before he could kill another fellow guard. Some people were made for war. Cathal hadn't realized how good he was at it until he became a Reaper. It wasn't that he enjoyed taking someone's life. It was quite the opposite, actually.

But there was something about fighting on the side of good to set the balance right again that made everything clear. Easy, even. He was working his way through a line of attackers when he felt a stinging pain in his side. Cathal glanced down to find blood trickling from a wound.

The injury was small. Since no one could see him, it was likely just a lucky shot from somewhere. He didn't think anything about it as he continued his annihilation. It wasn't long before he fell to one knee, however. This time when he looked down, the wound was center mass on his thigh. That wasn't a chance shot. It had been taken on purpose.

As a Reaper, he healed quicker than a Fae, but it wouldn't be fast enough. Cathal climbed to his feet, gritting his teeth from the pain. Then he looked around, trying to figure out who was aiming at him—and how.

Seconds ticked by with nothing. He stood still, a perfect target for someone trying to aim for him. Unless…he narrowed his gaze as he studied every face. Still, he found nothing, but he had a theory. He moved to an attacker near him and punched the man in the face, knocking him down.

Immediately, an orb came flying right at the spot where Cathal stood. He moved to the side, letting it pass. Someone had figured out that he was veiled, and they were waiting to see where someone went down seemingly on their own, allowing them to take their shot. It was smart. Almost too clever.

And if they could do that to him, they could do it to Aisling. He hurriedly scanned the area for her. As soon as he spotted her, he jumped to her location and grabbed her, swinging her away right as a ball of magic came at her.

"What the actual fek?" Aisling asked as she looked at the orb.

Cathal met her red eyes. "Someone figured out what we're doing."

"But…how?" she asked.

He shrugged. "Perhaps we can ask that after we find the arsehole."

"It'll make keeping the attackers back more difficult."

"It's a challenge I'm up for," he said with a smile.

Her lips lifted in a grin. "Let's get to it, then."

It was all Sorcha could do to remain in the house. She debated whether to go back up to her father's room, but decided to respect his wishes. No doubt her uncle was with him, which explained why no one had come to check on her.

She hated not being able to see Cathal and make sure he was all right. Then again, the fact that he could remain veiled gave him an advantage. She wouldn't like it if he were fighting against her, but she certainly enjoyed it when he was on her side. There were so many questions she wanted answers to regarding Cathal. Her father's reaction to hearing that he'd died but was alive kept running through her head.

It had sounded odd when Cathal had told her that before, but then again, she knew very little about the Fae. For all she knew, there was a magical way they could be killed and come back. It wasn't as if the Skye Druids had classes on the Fae. Everyone knew the basics, and that was it.

She felt safe with Cathal and Aisling. Not once had she thought that she was in danger or that they meant her harm. Then there was the fact that she had fallen for Cathal. Hard. She used to laugh off love at first sight, right up until she experienced it herself. It existed, and she was proof of that.

Twisting her hands nervously, Sorcha thought she spotted where Aisling or Cathal might be. A couple of the attackers looked as if they'd tripped over the air and went down hard, not moving again. There was a smile on her face as she silently cheered Cathal and Aisling on. And, if she were honest, she wished she could be out there helping them.

But she hadn't done magic in ten years, and she couldn't be veiled. Those things kept her sidelined. Though, the truth was that she had no clue what to do in such a battle. Being a Halfling didn't automatically instill such knowledge in her. Fighting was learned, and she didn't have any skills.

Her thoughts skidded to a halt when she saw an orb of magic land where she believed either Cathal or Aisling might be. Two more balls of magic alit in quick succession, landing near the first. It was almost as if the first strike had painted a target for the others, because that's where the orbs began to condense.

A knot of foreboding settled in her stomach. All this time, she believed that Cathal and Aisling were nearly invincible because they could stay veiled. Now, she wasn't so sure. Thinking he could remain invisible and safe had allowed her to imagine that Cathal could always be hers. After all, he had been killed and was still walking around now. To her mind, it meant he couldn't die. She was coming to understand that she'd had a false sense of security regarding Cathal.

And the idea that she might lose him sent her spiraling into an abyss of fear and panic.

Cathal tried to get to his feet and move out of the way of the incoming orbs of magic, but his body wouldn't listen to him. He finally gave up trying to stand and just rolled out of the way. It was a good thing, too, because several more balls of magic landed where he had been. He didn't want to think about what would've happened had he still been there.

He was a Reaper with some of Death's magic in him that heightened his senses and increased his power, but that didn't mean he couldn't be killed. The fact that most Fae didn't even realize the Reapers were real kept them from being singled out or hunted. Yet something was going on now, and he didn't like it at all.

A part of him wanted to call for the other Reapers for help, but if someone at this battle knew what he and Aisling were, then he would only succeed in bringing his brethren into a slaughter. It was better if the others didn't know.

He managed to get on his hands and knees. Fae lay dead all around him. More and more of the guards at the manor were being killed now that he and Aisling had been sidelined. Cathal looked up and searched for Aisling to find her leaning against the building, wounded. He couldn't tell how badly she was hurt, but the fact that she had taken refuge told him she was in pain.

His gaze lifted to the upper floors of the manor. He didn't want Sorcha's father to die, but once his life was over, then those after her would cease in their attacks. The use of poison on a Fae wasn't very common. In fact, it was rare. Mostly because poison of any kind had a unique and horrifying effect on the Fae. They could last for days in pain as their bodies desperately tried to heal the toxin until the body finally gave up. He'd never seen a Fae who had been poisoned, but he'd heard about it. It took someone truly evil to kill a Fae in such a way.

"Cathal!"

The sound of his name on Aisling's lips brought his head up. Her expression told him that he had to get moving. He glanced over his shoulder to find a group of five Fae advancing on his location. Two of them wore the navy uniform of the manor guards, while the others were in regular clothes. The Fae were a mixture of Light and

Dark, both male and female. Something about the way they carried themselves said they knew they were powerful and dared anyone to challenge them. He'd seen something similar not so long ago.

That's when he realized who they were. These were the Fae trying to become something similar to the Others. And they had somehow managed to immobilize both him and Aisling.

Cathal didn't know if they were here for him and Aisling or for Sorcha. Frankly, he didn't care. He wasn't going to allow any of them to be taken. Especially Sorcha. She didn't deserve such a fate after everything that had happened to her family.

Gathering as much strength as he could, Cathal got to his feet and faced the group of Fae. The few remaining manor guards were still fighting others and had no idea what was going on. If one of them had to die, it would be him. Aisling was closer to Sorcha and could get her out.

He didn't look to the manor, even though he wanted one last look at his Halfling. She had been a bright light in his life, one he had briefly basked in. If she had brought him such joy in just a few days, he could only imagine how things would've been had they had decades together.

But that wasn't to be. He'd done unspeakable wrongs, and while Death had given him a second chance, in the end, he had to pay the price for the lives he'd taken. There must always be a balance, and his time had come.

With the image of Sorcha smiling up at him after they'd made love in his mind, he dropped his veil. The leader of the group—the same Fae who had tried to convince Sorcha that he was her father—smiled as he formed an orb of magic.

CHAPTER TWENTY-ONE

"No!" Sorcha shouted when she saw Cathal lower his veil.

No one heard her because of the sounds of battle. Her stomach dropped to her feet when she spotted the group of five Fae headed straight for Cathal. She scanned the area, hoping to see Aisling or at least some sign of her. But there was nothing.

Sorcha knew she didn't stand a chance against the Fae. She also knew that Cathal and Aisling had done everything to keep her protected. Yet she couldn't stand there and watch either of them die. For all she knew, Aisling might already be dead.

The attackers' numbers were dwindling, but then again, so were the manor guards'. She wasn't sure who would win. All of this was happening because of her. Fae were dying—because of her. She wouldn't allow Cathal's life to be taken.

She took a deep breath and moved from her hiding spot to the doorway. Then she walked out of the house.

"Sorcha!"

She looked to the side where she'd heard Aisling's voice. The Dark must be veiled, not that she blamed Aisling at all. "It's fine."

"Get back in the house."

Sorcha ignored the disembodied voice and kept walking. She hoped to catch everyone's attention to give Cathal and Aisling time to get away. But that's not what happened. The Fae headed toward Cathal and didn't take their eyes off him. She walked faster, heading straight for the Dark. Surely, someone would notice her.

When the clear leader of the group formed an orb of magic between his hands, Sorcha began running. If only she could teleport, but she didn't have that ability. She watched with a mixture of distress and terror as all five Fae shot balls of power at Cathal.

Move out of the way! She screamed in her mind. But Cathal remained where he was.

Right before the magic slammed into him, he was jerked out of the way. Sorcha knew Aisling had intervened. She'd have to thank the Dark female later. Right now, she was more concerned with making sure Cathal got away before he was killed.

To her surprise, the five Fae began hurling orb after orb at and around Cathal. Sorcha realized they were trying to get whoever had helped him. Despite Aisling's attempt, Sorcha could tell that the female was being pummeled with magic and unable to get away. So was Cathal. It was the last straw for her.

Sorcha halted about ten meters from the group, who were so focused on Cathal and Aisling that they had no idea there was someone about to unleash ten years of anger on them. She planted her feet and let her magic swamp her.

For the first time, she felt a difference in her power. She could actually discern what was Fae and what was Druid. And when they mixed, it was a heady, intoxicating feeling that made her lightheaded. The more she accepted the magic, the stronger it became until her entire body hummed with it.

It was unlike anything she'd ever felt before. Whether it was because it had been a decade since she'd called to it, or because she now knew about her Fae blood, there was something distinctly different about the magic now. And she liked it. A lot.

The force of the power was so intense that it felt as if she were doing everything she could to keep her feet on the ground. She wanted to control the magic, but she was running out of time. Cathal was covered in blood and burns from the orbs that kept slamming into his body. He fought to get up, and she saw his lips moving. No doubt, he urged Aisling to do the same.

The two most powerful Fae she knew had been brought low. Because of her. That made her sick to her stomach. Her gaze swung to the five Fae who stood with smiles on their faces as they rained their deadly magic down on her friends.

A calm descended over Sorcha, pushing aside her wrath and trepidation. It was almost as if she'd detached from herself. Like she was staring at the scene, looking at herself in the third person. She didn't question any of it as she raised her hands before her. With a battle cry that would make any Skye Druid proud, she threw her magic at the five Fae.

Shock reverberated through her when they went flying like bowling pins. As the two nearest her landed, unmoving, she saw that her magic had torn a hole through their centers. The other three fell to the ground, writhing in pain.

She advanced on them. She had never felt such hatred before. Sorcha halted next to the first one she reached and looked down at the female who was now missing an arm. The Light had fear in her eyes as she silently pleaded with Sorcha.

"You wanted to kill my friends," she told the Light. "Why should I show you any mercy?"

"Please," the woman said, her voice filled with agony.

Sorcha lifted her hand, ready to end the Fae, when someone gently took hold of her arm and turned her. She found herself staring into crimson eyes she knew well. Relief swept through her to find Cathal on his feet. She could tell that he was still in pain, but he was alive and standing before her.

He said nothing as he cupped her cheeks in his hands and searched her face. She didn't know what it was that he looked for, and it didn't matter. She smiled up at him, happier than she ever imagined. Yet, as each second passed, she began to fully comprehend what it was that she had within her grasp. The more she thought about Cathal leaving and never coming back, the more she knew that she would never forgive herself if she didn't tell him how she felt.

Just as her lips parted, a shout came from Aisling. Sorcha and Cathal turned their heads toward the female to find the leader of the Fae group and one other teleporting away. When Sorcha looked down at the Fae she'd been about to kill, she saw that the Light had died.

"You could've been killed," Cathal said. "Why didn't you stay in the manor?"

Sorcha cocked her head at him. "I left because I couldn't let you or Aisling die."

"But," he began.

Whatever he had been about to say faded as Aisling collapsed. They rushed to the Dark. Sorcha winced as she noted the wounds covering Aisling's body. Then she looked at Cathal and saw that his were even worse. Sorcha had no idea how Cathal was still standing.

He checked Aisling's pulse and then lifted her into his arms. As he stood, his gaze found Sorcha's. "I've got to get Aisling help."

"Of course," she urged.

But if she'd thought he might take her with him, she was wrong. Sorcha found herself standing alone with only a handful of manor guards still standing. She swallowed and turned around to retrace her steps to the house. She wasn't sure what to do. Should she return to Scotland? Stay here?

It was one thing to arrive by teleportation. She couldn't exactly get back the way she'd come. And she didn't want to ask her father or uncle for help either. Sorcha decided to walk the grounds and lose herself in the vast garden behind the manor as she thought about Cathal. She didn't want to worry whether or not she'd see him again. There was a very real chance that she wouldn't.

Whoever he and Aisling were, they weren't normal Fae. She sighed wistfully as she looked at the sky to see the sun beginning its descent. Sorcha wasn't sure what her life would be like from here on out, but she knew she would never be the same. The person who had locked herself away in her home for a decade was no more.

CHAPTER TWENTY-TWO

The moment Cathal arrived on Death's realm, he teleported straight to the white tower and bellowed for Erith and Cael. The two appeared immediately.

"What the hell happened?" Cael demanded as Cathal laid Aisling down on a table.

Cathal rested his hands on the table as he struggled to keep standing. "The Fae group of Others."

Erith's lavender eyes studied him as she frowned. "Sit."

"I need to get back to Sorcha," he said. As he pushed away from the table, the world went black.

Erith watched over both Cathal and Aisling for the next day as their bodies mended. Cael insisted on helping things along and used his newfound power to heal them. She knew her Reapers would survive, but she couldn't help but worry. There was more to the story that Cathal hadn't been able to tell her before he passed out.

The news that the Fae group like the Others had been responsible for the injury to her Reapers left her furious.

"How are they?" Eoghan asked as he entered the chamber.

Erith lifted her head and regarded him. Out of the corner of her eye, she saw Cael watching her. "Their bodies are healing."

"But?" Eoghan pressed.

Cael blew out a breath. "There was something different about the magic used against them. It was…very potent."

Potent enough to take down a Reaper. Nothing should've been able to do that to her family.

"They're here and healing. That's good news," Eoghan said. He clasped his hands behind his back. "The rest of my group is eager to locate the Fae responsible for this."

Erith shook her head. "Not yet. I'm not going to rush into anything until we figure out what the group is, who is leading them, and what they want."

"Seems pretty clear. They wanted to kill two Reapers," Cael pointed out.

Eoghan's black brows drew together. "The only reason Cathal and Aisling were in Scotland was because of the Halfling. Do you think it has anything to do with her?"

"I think we should ask Cathal," Cael said.

Erith's gaze jerked to Cathal to find his eyes open and watching her. She rose and went to stand beside him. "How do you feel?"

"Better than before," he replied as he sat up and swung his legs over the side of the bed.

Eoghan nodded to Cathal. "Good to have you back. Care to tell us what happened?"

"How is Aisling?" Cathal asked instead as he peered past Erith to the bed behind her.

She glanced at Aisling before meeting Cathal's gaze. "She's healing quickly. She'll be fine. Now, I think it's time you tell us everything."

Cathal blew out a breath as he ran a hand down his face. Then he began his story. Erith had known there was something about the Halfling. Otherwise, she wouldn't have drawn Cathal's attention. But Erith would never have guessed Sorcha's connection.

As Erith listened to Cathal's story, she realized that he had feelings for the Halfling, especially given the things he *wasn't* telling them. She didn't point that out, and neither did Cael or Eoghan. They waited until he finished his retelling before any of them said anything.

"She had that kind of power?" Eoghan asked in surprise.

Cathal raised his brows as he nodded. "I've never seen anything like it. It was… pure. I don't even think Sorcha realizes what is within her grasp."

"Did her stepmother know, you think?" Cael asked.

Erith shook her head. "I don't think I've ever known of a Halfling who is half Skye Druid. The combination of two powerful families created Sorcha and her magic."

"She seemed surprised by it," Cathal told them. "And based on her story, she never had that kind of magic before."

Erith exchanged a look with Cael before she told Cathal, "Sorcha always had that kind of power. It wasn't until she needed it that she was able to use it."

Cathal frowned. "That isn't true. She could've used that power to save her mother and sister."

"You misunderstand Death," Eoghan said. "Sorcha came to your defense."

Cathal paused for a moment before he jerked his chin to Aisling. "Not just me."

"It was you. Trust me," Cael said.

Erith watched the play of emotions cross the Reaper's face. She wondered if Cathal knew that he was in love with Sorcha. Some

Reapers were loud and boisterous, and others were quiet. Usually, it was the quiet ones who had suffered the most. Eoghan had been such a Reaper. So was Cathal.

As for Aisling, her pain was a hundred times what any other Reaper had ever endured.

"How long have I been unconscious?" Cathal asked.

Cael said, "A day."

"I need to see Sorcha."

Erith issued a nod. "I assumed you would."

"I'd...I would like..." Cathal dropped his chin to his chest and grew quiet.

Erith looked at Eoghan and Cael and waited for them to leave. Once she was alone with Cathal, she walked to the bed and sat beside him. Neither of them spoke for several minutes. Finally, she said, "I know what you want to ask."

"I'm afraid you'll refuse me," he said without looking at her.

In all her time with Cathal, she had never known him to be afraid of anything. To hear him admit that now proved just how much he loved Sorcha. "You don't want to ask it because I've let the other Reapers have the women they love by saying those women have proven themselves to me. By helping us out against Bran or aiding a fellow Reaper."

"Aye."

"What do you think Sorcha did? Had she not stepped in and used her magic, it's very likely both you and Aisling might have been killed."

Cathal's head turned so that he looked at her. "You've not asked why I didn't call for help."

"Because you knew the Fae Others were after you, and you didn't want any other Reapers to be hurt," she said.

Cathal blew out a breath and nodded. "It almost got Aisling killed."

"You don't just have a team, Cathal. You have a family. You felt that about the others, but I think you've come to realize they think that about you, as well." She got to her feet and faced him. "Sorcha is waiting for you. It's up to you what you tell her. As for me, you have my blessing to tell her who you are."

"What if she says she doesn't want to be with me?"

Only a fool would pass up someone like Cathal. In fact, she felt that way about all her Reapers. They had all been betrayed and killed. She had given them a second life, and by doing so, had given all of them—including herself—a family. She would protect each of her Reapers with her very life.

"You'll never find out if you don't go see her," Erith said with a smile.

Cathal nodded as he got to his feet. He looked at her and grinned. "Thank you."

As she watched him walk out of the room and down the stairs of the tower, she hoped that Sorcha wanted Cathal, as well. No one had refused a Reaper yet. She wasn't sure what she would do when that time came—because it would. Maybe she could take a page from the Dragon Kings and wipe the person's memory of anything having to do with the Reapers.

It was either that or kill the person. Because no one could know about the Reapers or her. It put everything they were and what they did in jeopardy.

Cael filled the doorway. He leaned a shoulder against it and crossed his arms over his chest. "It looks like we've got to find out how the Fae Others discovered the Reapers."

"I know," she said as she walked to him.

Just when she thought they might have some peace, a new enemy reared its head. And they still hadn't had any luck finding Xaneth. She was losing hope when it came to the Light Fae. He'd been a friend, and she had promised to find him and free him. Save him from his aunt, Usaeil. However, if she didn't find him soon, it might be too late for the royal Fae.

CHAPTER TWENTY-THREE

Sorcha stood in the garden. Her tears had dried. Even knowing that her father was dying hadn't stopped the grief when the poison finally took him. At the funeral, she'd met his side of the family. She hadn't been prepared for how large it was.

At some point, she would have to tell Rhona everything. She'd spoken to her cousin to let her know that she wasn't on Skye, and while Rhona had asked several questions, Sorcha had asked for some time before she answered them.

A gentle breeze ruffled the flowers. Sorcha was still getting used to having an entire manor to herself. She'd been content with her little cottage. Yet she'd be lying if she said she didn't love the manor and the estate. Maybe it was because it had been her father's and the home he'd wanted to give to her mother. Or perhaps it was because it had been the last place she'd seen Cathal.

She had tried not to think of him, but it was a losing battle. Cathal invaded her thoughts constantly. She wondered where he was and if he and Aisling were all right. He hadn't said he would come back. She tried not to hold out hope that he would, but she couldn't seem to help herself. Even with the knowledge that a new life awaited her, she kept reliving the time she'd had with Cathal.

"You look fetching among the flowers."

At the sound of his voice, she stilled, her heart thumping wildly. Sorcha spun around to find him standing behind her. His long hair was pulled back in a queue. All his wounds looked healed, and he had a smile on his face. She wanted to run to him, but she held herself in check. "Apparently, this is my home now."

He nodded. "It suits you." Then he frowned. "I'm sorry about your father."

"Thanks," she said and glanced away. The silence grew awkward, so she searched for something to say. "How is Aisling?"

"She's good. Healing."

"As did you."

He glanced down at himself and shrugged. "You saved us. I still can't believe you did that. I can't thank you enough."

"After everything you did for me…" she said with a smile. "You don't ever need to thank me for anything."

"I disagree," he said as he took a step toward her.

She moved closer to him. "It's good to see you."

"It's really good to see you." He took another step.

Sorcha bit her lip and found herself closing the distance between them. "I wasn't sure I'd ever see you again."

"I would've been here sooner, but I was still healing." With one last step, he bridged the gap between them. "There is something I want to tell you."

She nodded. "Sure. Anything."

His lips parted, but instead of talking, his arms snaked out and pulled her against him. The feeling of his lips moving over hers made Sorcha moan. She wound her arms around his neck and pressed her body against his, sinking into the desire that erupted between them.

Unfortunately, he ended the kiss as quickly as he had begun it. Cathal pressed his forehead to hers, his eyes squeezed closed. "You never asked me why I could do all the things I can. You simply accepted it without question."

She smoothed her hand down his cheek. "Did you want me to ask?"

"I don't know," he said as he opened his eyes to look at her. "The fact you accepted who I am without question isn't something I'm used to."

Sorcha smiled as she shrugged. "I knew you'd tell me if you could."

"I'm a Reaper."

She blinked, unsure if she was supposed to know what that was. "All right," she finally said.

Cathal took her hand and led her to a bench. He sat and pulled her down beside him. "What I'm about to tell you isn't something anyone can know. If a Fae discovers this information, Death kills them."

"Death." Now that got Sorcha's attention.

Cathal looked away briefly. "I told you about my stepmother's betrayal and my death. Death comes to some of those who are betrayed after their souls leave their bodies. We're offered a second life, if you will. We get to live, but we become Reapers. Death is the judge and jury for the Fae, we're the executioners."

"Reapers," Sorcha said with a nod. "Now, I understand. You reap Fae souls."

"Exactly. Most Fae think we're myths. That's how Death wants it. If the Fae discover who we are, they'll try to blackmail us or get us to help them."

Sorcha could well imagine that. "Makes sense."

"When Death gives us back our souls once we agree to service, we have added power, enhancements to our magic that allows us to do things other Fae can't."

"Like remain veiled for as long as you want," Sorcha said.

Cathal grinned. "My life is dedicated to Death and the other Reapers. I obey Death in all things."

The hope Sorcha felt at hearing Cathal's story quickly diminished. "Are you telling me all of this because you can't be with me?"

"I'm telling you this because I want to be with you. I want to spend my life with you. But you need to understand that it's going to be different. For one, we don't live on this realm. We live on another that only we can get to."

She hadn't expected that. Then again, it made complete sense.

Cathal hesitated, his gaze searching hers. "I know we've not known each other long, but I know how I feel. If you nee—"

"I love you," she said over him.

He blinked, then a smile broke over his face. "I love *you*."

She flung herself into his arms and held onto him. "I don't care where I live, as long as I get to be with you."

"Are you sure? I don't know if—or when—you'll be able to see your family again."

Sorcha thought about that for a moment. "This is my father's home. It's the place he and my mother were supposed to be. As much as I like it here, it's not mine. I know it's my inheritance, but others in the family probably deserve it more than I do."

"It was meant to protect you. His wife would never be able to harm you here."

Sorcha nodded slowly. "As for Skye, it's the only home I've ever known. It was my mother's land, and I stayed because I punished myself. I've not been a part of the Skye Druids in a long time. And now, knowing that I'm a Halfling…I don't feel as if I belong there anymore."

A slight frown marred Cathal's brow. "Do you understand that you can't tell anyone where you're going if you come with me?"

"I do. All I've thought about these last few days is you and what a life with you would be like. Granted, I didn't know you were a Reaper, but I don't care. I want my life to be with you, whatever that entails and wherever that is."

Cathal touched her face gently. "I've never been happier than I am in this moment. Tell me when you're ready, and we'll go."

"I've got some things to do before we can. First, I need to relinquish everything my father gave me. Then, I need to speak to Rhona."

Cathal bowed his head, a smile still in place. "All right."

"Will you come with me?"

"I always want to be with you."

It didn't take long for Sorcha to find Eddie and tell him that she needed to relinquish her inheritance. There were questions in her uncle's eyes, but after he glanced at Cathal, it seemed he decided to keep them to himself. In less than two hours, everything that Sorcha had gained through her father had been divided up between the rest of her relatives—which were numerous.

It felt good—and right—to hand it all back. Not that she didn't want any of it. She very much did. But she couldn't see herself living in Ireland, even though her father had done everything in his power to keep her safe. She would love him forever for that. She didn't need the material possessions to remember him.

As she walked out of the manor holding Cathal's hand, she glanced over her shoulder at it one more time. "I wonder what my life would've been like had my mother been able to marry my father."

"I think you would've been loved, just as you were."

She smiled at him. "You're right."

"Ready to go to Skye?"

She swallowed and gave him a nod. In the next instant, they were at her cottage. It felt as if she had been gone for years, not days. Sorcha used her mobile and called Rhona to ask her cousin to come and visit. While she waited, Sorcha walked through the house, letting the memories fill her—and taking the bad with the good.

"We don't have to do this now," Cathal said.

She turned around as she stood in her bedroom and found him

leaning against the doorframe. "It's time. I think I realized I needed to move on when Rhona sent me to Ireland to spy for her. I tried to deny it, but it was there all along."

Cathal's head jerked around at the sound of a car door.

"Don't veil yourself," Sorcha said as she grabbed his hand on her way to the front of the house.

She opened the door before Rhona could reach it. Her cousin's green eyes went straight to Cathal.

"Hello," Rhona said hesitantly.

Sorcha stepped aside to let her cousin enter. "Thanks for coming. There are some things you need to know."

Rhona said nothing as she walked into the house and turned to face them. "You mean that you're half-Fae."

"What?" Sorcha asked in surprise.

Rhona shrugged, her lips twisting as she cut her eyes to Cathal. "Sorry. I saw him and realized that you must know the truth now."

"How long have you known?" Cathal asked Rhona.

Her cousin pressed her lips together. "My mum told me before she died. She made it sound as if you already knew, so I didn't bring it up."

"I don't understand." Sorcha moved to the chair so she could hold onto it. "How did you know? I just learned of it a few days ago from Cathal. Mum didn't even tell me."

"Your mum and mine had lunch together about a week before the accident," Rhona said. "Apparently, your mum told mine everything about your father and how he was Light Fae."

Sorcha blinked rapidly to keep the tears from spilling over her eyes. "I got to meet him before he died. It's a long story, but he had a wife that he wanted to divorce for mum, but the woman wouldn't let him. She was the one who killed Mum and Molly."

Rhona rushed to her and enveloped Sorcha in a hug. "I'm so sorry. But you have to know, none of us ever blamed you."

"I know." Sorcha sniffed and dashed the tears away before she pulled back. "And thank you for that."

"So," Rhona said as she looked between Sorcha and Cathal. "I'm guessing this means you're leaving."

Sorcha smiled and took Cathal's hand. "Rhona, this is Cathal. And, yes. I am leaving with him to start a new life. I'm not sure when I'll be back."

"It's nice to meet you, Cathal," Rhona said with a smile. "If you hurt my cousin, I'll find you and cut out your heart."

There was a wide smile on Cathal's face when he said, "You won't ever have to do that, but I respect you more because you said it."

"And this house will always be yours," Rhona told Sorcha. "We'll keep it up in case you ever need a place to go."

Sorcha hugged Rhona again. "I love you, and I'm going to miss you."

"Same." Rhona sniffed and quickly turned her head away to hide the tears. When she had herself under control, she looked back at them. "So, is this farewell?"

"For now," Cathal said.

Sorcha suddenly looked at Cathal. "Before the Others were defeated, Rhona and many Druids here fought Moreann."

"Just proves how powerful all of you are," Cathal said to Rhona. Then he blinked. "Wait. You're the Druids who found Moreann?"

Rhona nodded with a smile. "That was us, yes. Thanks to Corann leading us to her."

"That means you know where Usaeil was."

Sorcha felt the tension vibrating off Cathal. She wasn't sure what was going on, but whatever it was, it was important.

Rhona was more hesitant now as she said, "We did."

Cathal took a step toward her, his chest rising and falling rapidly. "Did you find a Fae there named Xaneth? He's Usaeil's nephew. She captured him months ago. We've been looking for him ever since."

"We looked through the entire estate. We didn't find any Light Fae there. Only Usaeil's Trackers," Rhona told him.

Cathal sighed heavily. "It was worth a shot to think that Xaneth might be there."

Sorcha frowned as she looked at her cousin. "Can you give us the location? Perhaps it'll be good for Cathal and his friends to walk around the place."

"That's a great idea," he said.

Rhona flashed them a smile and told them where she'd found Usaeil.

EPILOGUE

Cathal had never been so nervous as he was to take Sorcha to Death's realm. He couldn't take his eyes from her as they walked through the doorway into the new world. Sorcha's eyes widened as her mouth dropped open. She hurried from plant to plant, touching the leaves and inhaling the fragrance of the flowers.

He simply stood back with a smile on his face.

"Well, that's not something I thought I'd ever see," Eoghan said as he walked up. "A genuine smile."

Cathal nodded as he glanced at the leader before he jerked his chin to Sorcha. "It's all because of her."

"We're all very eager to meet her. Especially Erith."

Cathal didn't want to spoil Sorcha's fun, but they did have years for her to enjoy the flowers. He called out to her, and she turned to him with a smile. As she approached, she shot Cathal a bright smile. "There is heather by the water. I can't believe it." Then she held out her hand to Eoghan and said, "Hi. I'm Sorcha."

"Hello, Sorcha. I'm Eoghan."

Cathal leaned down and whispered, "My boss."

Sorcha's emerald eyes widened. "Ah. I see. It is a pleasure to meet you."

"Come," Eoghan told them. "The others are waiting for you."

Cathal felt the faint tremor in Sorcha's hand, but she eagerly walked with him. As they approached the white tower, she began to relax. It had been the same for him the first time he'd seen the structure. There was just something about it.

Sorcha was in awe. Everywhere she looked was a beauty so glorious she couldn't find words. The moment they reached the tower and walked inside, a petite woman with long, blue-black hair stepped forward. She was clothed in a gown of all black, and her lavender eyes were framed by long, thick lashes. She had to be the most stunning creature Sorcha had ever seen. Without a doubt, Sorcha knew this was Death.

"It's nice to have you here with us, Sorcha. I hope you like your new home. I'm Erith, but outside of this realm, you will refer to me as Death," she said. Then she motioned to a Light Fae with purple eyes. "And this is my husband and mate, Cael."

Sorcha swallowed, nodding. "Thank you for allowing me here. I'll love Cathal with all my heart for the rest of my days."

"We know," Eoghan said. "Otherwise, you wouldn't be here."

Then, one by one, she was introduced to the rest of Cathal's team and their mates before the first team of Reapers came forward. There was no way she would remember everyone's name, but that didn't matter. She knew she'd found her home here with Cathal and the Reapers.

A day later…

Cathal stood with Sorcha and the rest of his team of Reapers in what was left of Usaeil's home, where she had taken Moreann, Corann, and the other Druids. But Xaneth wasn't here. It wasn't until Sorcha nudged him and pointed to Aisling, who stood near a doorway looking into a room, that they walked to her. Cathal looked over Aisling to find a bed and the impression of a body on the mattress, as well as a headprint on the pillow.

"He was here," Aisling said softly.

Eoghan pushed past her and walked into the room. After just a few seconds, he called Death's name. Erith and Cael immediately appeared.

Death's lavender gaze locked on the bed before she nodded. "Xaneth was here," she confirmed.

"Then where the hell is he now?" Rordan asked.

Torin crossed his arms over his chest and shrugged. "He must have been held here. It makes sense since no one could locate Usaeil when she was here."

"And what?" Bradach asked. "Usaeil's magic faded upon her death, and he was able to leave?"

Cael walked to the bed and put his hand upon it. He jerked back almost immediately as his gaze snapped to Erith. She joined him. Together, they put their hands on the mattress. Death hissed in a breath, but she didn't pull back. It was Cael who took hold of her and physically moved her away from the bed.

He held her silently for a moment before he looked at each of them. "Usaeil's magic held Xaneth. She had him trapped in his own mind."

Aisling turned her back to the room. Then, with a shuddering breath, she walked away without a word. Cathal watched her go before he turned his attention to Cael.

"Xaneth got free on his own," Erith told the room.

Rordan winced. "Fek me."

"We need to find him soon," Dubhan stated.

Eoghan nodded. "It's time to get back to our realm and start planning."

Death gave a nod. "Unfortunately, now that the Druids of Ireland have decided to create their own group of Others, things may go the same on Skye."

"My cousin doesn't want that," Sorcha said. "But it may be out of her hands."

Torin blew out a breath. "Just when we thought things with the Others was over."

"We'll get a handle on it," Cael said.

Someone was going to die. It was the only way Xaneth could stop this hell he was living in. He just needed to find the right person.

Continue reading for a sneak peek at **Dark Alpha's Obsession**, the next book in the Reapers series.

EXCERPT OF DARK ALPHA'S OBSESSION
REAPERS SERIES, BOOK 11

Achill Island, Ireland
End of July

Tonight was no different than the others. Same speech given by her brother. Same curious faces watching him. Same security in place.

But something was off.

Fianna couldn't put her finger on it no matter how many times she scanned the faces in the room. No one appeared out of place. Then again, few rarely did during the first meetings. Because that's what this was. The first of three before Dorcha chose which ones would be welcomed into their community.

She remained in the shadows, her eyes stopping to inspect each face of the thirty gathered. It was her duty to spot any trouble. And she was damned good at it. While her brother had been gifted a silver tongue that could enrapture a room with just a few words, her skills ran to battle, weapons, and magic. Since she detested being the center of attention, she was quite happy being head of security and staying in the background.

Movement out of the corner of her eye caught her attention. She turned her head and spotted her brother making his way from a back room to the makeshift stage that had been put in place just for him. Their gazes briefly met. Dorcha shot her a wink before he put a huge smile on his face and waved to the gathered crowd.

She had no idea how he did this night after night. He thrived on it, while the very thought of repeating the speeches made her want to gauge her eyes out. Then again, Dorcha couldn't understand why she loved to train daily or got such a thrill out of maintaining his security. They were, as their father often said, as different as night and day.

Fianna looked to the door to see a few late stragglers entering the manor just as her brother's voice filled the room. She paid no attention to her brother. Her job was on keeping an eye on those who attended. There were few who truly understood how important Dorcha was. But they would soon enough.

Hers and Dorcha's entire lives had led up to what was building. Fianna had trained tirelessly, became proficient at old magic that had been forgotten, and learned to fight with a unique set of weapons while Dorcha had absorbed knowledge from ancient scrolls and perfected his speaking voice.

She waited until the door closed behind the last individual before she made her way around the perimeter of the room. Their meeting place was in none other than Moorehall. It was a striking edifice with dark gray stone against the vibrant green surroundings. There were times, like now, when she looked upon the splendor of the manor that she felt sorry humans couldn't witness such breathtaking grandeur. Thanks to Fae magic, the mortals believed the manor was haunted and nothing but a crumbling house which had been neglected and forgotten.

Fianna moved slowly, keeping as far from the guests. Her security team was set up throughout the manor, hidden so as not to draw attention to themselves – or the fact that Dorcha even had security.

Once she made it all the way back to the other side of the stage, she set up in her usual spot and set about watching the crowd. With her brother's voice in the background, she noticed that nearly everyone laughed at his jokes, nodded their heads in agreement, or clapped with enthusiasm. Her attention locked on the three who did neither of those things.

Two males stood at the back with their arms crossed over their chests with a look of discontent on their faces. Their heads were tilted towards each other and they spoke in whispers, alerting her that they had most likely come together. She gave a nod to two of her men near her and jerked her chin to the pair she had observed. Her men would station themselves near the two individuals to intervene should it become necessary.

And sometimes, it was necessary.

People didn't always like what Dorcha had to say. But it needed said, and if he was the only one strong enough and brave enough to say it, then it fell to him.

Her gaze slid to the other guest who made no motion of agreement. The male Fae stood tall, his gaze direct as he watched Dorcha. Fianna leaned to the side to get a better view of the male. He wore a leather jacket over a black tee which prohibited her from seeing his physique. His thick black hair was trimmed short, the kind of cut a man wore when he didn't want to be bothered with styling his hair. He had a strong jawline, regal nose, and wide lips that were a full and utterly sexy.

Handsome? He was definitely that. But there was something else about him as well. A hint of danger, maybe? The fact she couldn't figure him out as she did others intrigued her.

He shifted slightly, taking a deep breath that lifted his shoulders as he stuffed his fingers into the front pockets of his jeans. She noticed his gaze moving about, as if he were sizing up those around him. Fianna was instantly on alert, though she had to remind herself that this meeting was one that led to something very secret. Perhaps this man suspected that and was just looking out for himself.

Her stomach fluttered when the Fae's lips suddenly turned up slightly in the corners. Fianna instinctively took a step back. She wanted to run to her room and put as much distance between them as she could, but that wasn't an option. Not now, at least.

She forced herself to hold her ground and look anywhere but his face. Little by little, she gained control of herself. It had been a long time since she had been so…overcome. And she was grateful that neither Dorcha nor her father had witnessed the episode. Yet, even when she had control of herself, she still didn't look at the Fae's face again. That would be idiotic, and she was anything but.

Continue Dark Alpha's Obsession, order today!

ABOUT THE AUTHOR

New York Times and *USA Today* bestselling author Donna Grant has been praised for her "totally addictive" and "unique and sensual" stories. She's written more than one hundred novels spanning multiple genres of romance including the *New York Times* bestselling *Dark Kings* series featuring immortal Highlander shape shifting dragons who are daring, untamed, and seductive. She lives with her two children, two dogs, and four cats in Texas.

www.DonnaGrant.com
www.MotherofDragonsBooks.com

THANK YOU!

Thank you for reading **DARK ALPHA'S CARESS**. I hope you enjoyed it! If you liked this book – or any of my other releases – please consider rating the book at the online retailer of your choice. Your ratings and reviews help other readers find new favorites, and of course there is no better or more appreciated support for an author than word of mouth recommendations from happy readers. Thanks again for your interest in my books!

Donna Grant
www.DonnaGrant.com
www.MotherofDragonsBooks.com